"Now, about the pipe," he said patiently

"The pipe to carry the water down to the house and make everything peachy clean."

"Oh, that." She shook her head, sighing. "That has to wait, Steady. We just don't have the money right now. *Poco a poco*, a little at a time, that's the way we have to do things."

"Sounds like a good idea," he returned. "*Poco a poco*. I must remember that phrase. Now, do we shake hands or do I get to kiss you?"

"Oh Lord, no!" She backed away as he slowly stalked her across the kitchen. Finally with her back up against the sink, his arms came down one on each side of her.

"Oh no, what?" he asked, his voice barely a whisper. "No kiss, or no handshake?"

EMMA GOLDRICK describes herself as a grandmother first and an author second. She was born and raised in Puerto Rico where she met her husband, a career military man from Massachusetts. His postings took them all over the world, which often led to mishaps—such as the Christmas they arrived in Germany before their furniture. Emma uses the places she's been as backgrounds for her books, but just in case she runs short of settings, this prolific author and her husband are always making new travel plans.

Books by Emma Goldrick

HARLEQUIN PRESENTS

688—AND BLOW YOUR HOUSE DOWN
791—MISS MARY'S HUSBAND
825—NIGHT BELLS BLOOMING
841—RENT-A-BRIDE LTD.
866—DAUGHTER OF THE SEA
890—THE OVER-MOUNTAIN
953—HIDDEN TREASURES
1035—IF LOVE BE BLIND
1087—MY BROTHER'S KEEPER
1208—MADELEINE'S MARRIAGE

HARLEQUIN ROMANCE

2661—THE ROAD
2739—THE TROUBLE WITH BRIDGES
2846—TEMPERED BY FIRE
2858—KING OF THE HILL
2889—TEMPORARY PARAGON
2943—TO TAME A TYCOON
2967—THE LATIMORE BRIDE
2984—PILGRIM'S PROMISE

EMMA GOLDRICK

a heart as big as texas

Harlequin Books

TORONTO • NEW YORK • LONDON
AMSTERDAM • PARIS • SYDNEY • HAMBURG
STOCKHOLM • ATHENS • TOKYO • MILAN

To my daughter Jeanne,
the best research assistant
this side of the San Andreas Fault

Harlequin Presents first edition July 1990
ISBN 0-373-11281-5

Original hardcover edition published in 1989
by Mills & Boon Limited

CHAPTER ONE

THE ditch was barely a scratch in the dry earth. Alison Springer slammed her shovel into the ground, set her foot up on it, and used one long sleeve of her old cotton blouse to wipe the perspiration out of her eyes. Not much progress, she told herself. Sixty yards from the head of the new well to the side of the house, and I've managed four. Is it deep enough? How far down does a water-pipe have to be buried to avoid a winter freeze in South Texas? She had never seen a freeze, and could not estimate.

She used herself as a measure. Five feet four inches tall, she had dug down until the lip of the ditch was at her chin. She pulled off her stetson and let the teasing wind play with her long brown hair for a moment before she stuffed it all back under her hat and bent to the task again. The pick was too heavy, but she swung it anyway, wincing as the point bounced off a rock and transmitted the shock up into her hand. 'That's all I need,' she muttered, rubbing her palm.

She stretched to her full height, turned slightly, and found herself face to face with an old Romney ewe. 'Git!' Alison yelled, and waved her hands. The sheep backed away, paused, was joined by another, and then surged forward to the edge of the ditch again. Allie shook her head in disgust. Sheep might not be the dumbest animals on the face of the earth, but her particular flock was close enough to the title to make do! Now there were six or more sweet, innocent little white faces peering out of a tangled mass of hornless rough grey Romney fleece. They followed her movements even as they chewed. And, given the slightest opportunity, she knew, they would jump or be pushed into the ditch with her. 'Scat!' she yelled. The sheep withdrew a foot or two, and stood their ground. Which means, Alison told herself grimly, that there's something behind them that bothers them more than I do!

She set both hands on the side of the ditch, and gave herself a little boost. The red dirt gave her no purchase; she managed a couple of inches, and then slipped back into the excavation. The denims that might once have been blue were now red-smeared. Two or three words came to mind. The kind a girl might learn while working beside a couple of ranch-hands. She tugged her hat back down on to her head and reached out for another grip.

'Give you a hand?' Alison shaded her eyes from the sun with one hand. There was a man, an indistinct figure in the glare of the sun, sitting easily in the saddle of the most beautiful palomino quarter-horse Allie had ever seen. She stared in awe, hardly noticing that the man was swinging down out of the saddle.

'Put her there, sonny.' A large hand, about as big as she had ever seen, was stretched out in her direction. 'Diggin' a hole?'

'No,' she muttered sarcastically as she grabbed at the proffered help. 'No, I hear the Panama Canal is choked with traffic. I'm building a second unit.'

His hand clenched on hers, and she was airborne, all one hundred and six pounds. When she landed with a thump she almost lost her balance, and careened forward into his arms. 'You didn't have to be so enthusiastic,' she told him. Her normally contralto voice was muffled because her head was buried in his fancy linen shirt.

He set her aside with a little chuckle. 'Your mother never taught you not to answer sassy? You don't look hardly big enough to be diggin' a canal. Your pa at home?'

About to give him a sassy answer, Alison put a clamp on her mouth. Even in South Texas it wasn't the smartest thing for a girl to tell a strange man that she was all alone in the middle of two hundred and forty acres, ten miles north of the San Antonio city limits. Instead of answering, she leaned back and glared up at him.

'Look,' he said with a sigh, 'your damn sheep are running all over my bottom land. Who's in charge?'

'Why don't we just ride up to the house?' The sweet soprano voice shocked Alison. She hadn't noticed the second rider, a tall, thin blonde of about thirty or so, sitting in an English saddle—good lord!—atop a magnificent thoroughbred roan. 'The kid evidently doesn't know to come in out of the rain!' The sarcasm bit, like the sting from the tail of a scorpion. Alison's sun-bronzed face turned a shade darker as she wrestled with her temper.

'No need to get abusive,' she muttered. 'They're only a couple of animals, not an invasion.' The sheep nuzzled against her, ignoring the gaping ditch. 'Well, *somebody* left the gate open,' she said. 'It wasn't Pablo. He's up on the north range with the young flock. And it wasn't Carmen. She's been down in the *barrio* overnight, having the kids checked out by Dr Miranda. And it wasn't me. I've been digging for this darn water-pipe since six this morning! There was some rackety rider down by the farm road about three hours ago, racing around like he had ants in his pants. Anybody you know?'

He looked at her, and then up at his companion. The blonde blushed. 'Not me,' she said, denying the accusation before it was made.

'No, I don't suppose it would be either of you,' Alison commented. 'But newcomers to the country have to remember that gates are important.'

She turned her attention back to the milling sheep. From sixty yards away on the veranda of the house, Michael managed to raise his hoary old muzzle. Alison inserted two fingers into her mouth and whistled. The sheep scattered; the old black and white dog came to his feet, running; the palomino pranced a step or two and was quickly controlled; the thoroughbred roan bucked, and almost threw its rider. And by that time the sheepdog was following Alison's hand signals, rounding up the Romneys and moving them up the hill and over the crest.

'Another time you might be more careful,' he said, one hand on the roan's bridle. 'We're not here to start another Range War. All I want to do is keep your—flock——' he hesitated just long enough to indicate a couple of unsaid words there '—from eating my mother's flower-bed. Very partial to flowers, my mother is.'

'Might at that,' Alison agreed, but contriteness had never been her cup of tea. She decided to take the offensive. 'My sheep wouldn't be on your bottom land if someone hadn't left the gate open down there. And what land are you talking about? There's nobody living within ten miles of this spread, as far as I know.'

He grinned at her. A big man, she noted. Not tall—just big in all directions. A square, strong face, sunburned, as if being out of doors was not his usual thing. A thatch of blond hair. Hazel eyes. Not handsome, but altogether impressive. 'Colson,' he introduced himself. 'Stedman Colson. Folks call me Steady. Make you known to Harriet Glebe.' He waved a casual hand in his companion's direction. 'I bought out the old Harrison place.'

'Springer,' she said, and then stopped to think. 'Al Springer.' Their two hands met again in a brief shake, hers swallowed up entirely by his. A firm hand, she thought. Strong, but gentle. Why in the world would he want to be seen with anyone named Harriet? But Texas hospitality required her to—— 'Come down to the house and have a cool drink,' she invited.

He nodded, grinning, and matched steps to hers, leaving the palomino to follow along. Harriet Glebe made no attempt to dismount, merely nudging her roan in their general direction. Not that I blame her, Alison thought. It's downright hot this morning, and she makes a pretty picture on that mount. Thoroughbreds both, from the look of it. Her short, curly blonde hair escaped from her riding cap in all directions. Her white silk blouse and tan jodhpurs—with spurs, no less—were just what a lady rancher might be seen wearing. In the pages of *Cosmopolitan*, that was, not out on the parched Texas range.

'Springer,' he mused. 'Used to be a Grannie Springer in these parts, years ago. Know of her?'

'Just might,' Alison said, stalling.

'She still around?'

'Some say one way, some say t'other. You a relative of hers?'

'Nope. When I was a tad I spent a summer down at the Harrison place. Grannie took me in hand. Taught me some manners—things like that. Never forget that kind of thing. That's why I came back.'

And, indeed, one never does, Allie told herself. If it hadn't been for Grannie—well, things would be terribly different for herself, for the Hernandez family, and certainly for the children!

She stopped short, meaning to say something cordial, but the palomino, following nose-to-shoulder, bumped into her, sending her sprawling in the sparse grass in front of the stairs. Her stetson went rolling with the wind.

'Well, and what have we here?' he asked, leaning down over her and offering that big hand again. 'Little boy or big girl? Which, I wonder? Al Springer?'

'Alison,' she muttered, levered up off the ground for the second time by that muscular hand. 'Alison Springer. Did you want to make something out of that?'

He backed off a step or two, grinning. 'Not me, lady,' he protested, holding up both hands defensively. 'I am the most peaceful cowpoke you ever met!'

It *must* have been a family joke. Harriet Glebe, swinging down gracefully from her mount, broke into laughter. Stedman Colson gave Harriet an injured look over his shoulder. 'You mustn't mind Miss Glebe,' he said. 'Lawyers have a strange sense of humour. She is an assistant prosecutor for Bexar County.'

If he had calmly announced that Harriet Glebe was the Devil's chief assistant, he could not have startled Alison more. She whirled around, back to both of them as she fumbled to tuck her blouse back into her denims. Assistant prosecutor? Dear lord in heaven! Her blouse was straight before her face was—she waited an added couple of seconds. 'Come in.' Her voice trembled, but there was nothing she could do about *that*. Guilty consciences were sometimes hard to hide.

'I'm sure you're both dying for something cool to drink,' she said.

The pair of them tethered their horses to the hitching post and clumped up the six stairs that led to the veranda.

*   *   *

'So—you are Grannie Springer's for-real grand-daughter?' He toasted her with a vague gesture of his lemonade glass.

'The only one left,' she acknowledged. 'Grannie died several years ago, and—well, things are as you see.'

'Nothing wrong with what I see.' He chuckled. 'House is a bit old, sure, but it's been many a year since I saw a floor polished so you could see your face in it.'

'And you live here all alone?' Harriet Glebe, settled comfortably in a captain's chair, had come down off both her horses—the roan and her 'high horse'.

'No, not exactly,' Allie said. 'Pablo is my shepherd, his wife Carmen is my housekeeper. They live in the west wing. And they have two adorable little babies. Lovely little creatures!'

'You sound as if you wished they were yours,' the lady lawyer commented.

'Good lord, yes. As fine a pair of children as I could wish for. But—some things are beyond reach.'

'Not for everybody,' Harriet Glebe said. 'That's just the sort of thing Steady and I are hoping for. A healthy, happy child.'

'Carts and horses, Harriet.' His voice had a touch of whiplash in it. Harriet flushed. She obviously knows exactly what he means, Alison thought. I wish I did.

'Then you two are going to get married?'

'We're—considering it,' he acknowledged. 'My mother——'

'If you brought home the Queen of Sheba your mother wouldn't approve,' Harriet interrupted sarcastically. 'Nothing's too good for the Lady of the Manor. And that's what you'll probably wind up with, Steady. Nothing!'

'No need to wash all the family linen in public,' he cautioned.

'But I'm not getting any younger, Steady,' she wailed.

'All right, all right.' He was doing his clumsy best to comfort her, but his heart was plainly not in it. After a moment he gave up.

'So you're putting in a new water-pipe, Alison?'

'If my back doesn't break,' she said. 'The old well is down in the flats. It held up during the drought, but now it's brackish. Frank Pillson was willing to drill a new well, what with oil-drilling being in such a poor state, but he couldn't see his way clear to throw in the pump and the pipes. I hired a couple of men from town to move the windmill over to the new site.' She gave a big sigh as she refilled the glasses. 'All I need is the pipeline.'

'Pablo can't help?'

'No. He was injured in the war, you know. He's a great shepherd, but there's not much else he can do— oh, odd jobs, truck-driving, that sort of thing. Last week we dipped the whole flock. I had to hire extra help for that.'

'Might take a look at it myself,' he said. 'Used to be a roustabout in the oilfields.'

'Damn it, Steady Colson!' Harriet Glebe was up on her feet, anger clouding her doll-perfect face. 'I thought we were going for a sociable ride. Now you're hiring out as a labourer!'

'It's just the sort of thing a neighbour would do.' He stood up, unfolding as gracefully as a ballet dancer. 'If you want to get back to the city, Harriet, why don't you go ahead? Frank will drive you. I'll pick you up around eight o'clock for the Bar Association dinner.'

Harriet tried one more appeal. 'I don't want Frank. I want you!'

He shrugged his shoulders. Harriet glared at him, then transferred her anger to Alison. 'This must be all the newest mode in seduction,' she said. 'Grubby sex? Well, see what *you* can make of him.' With which she slammed out of the house, and a moment later could be heard galloping off.

'She'll ruin that horse,' he said as he stared out of the window.

'I hope she shuts the gate,' Alison replied.

'Yeah, well, let me go have a look at your well.'

He moves like a tank, Alison thought as she watched. Or maybe a centre in the National Football league. Not exactly tall—perhaps five foot eleven or so—but built like a block of granite!

'Don't take Harriet at face value,' he said over his shoulder. 'She's a little disappointed by life. My mother wants me to get married, but *not* to Harriet. They'll both get over it.'

And what do you say to that? Alison asked herself. Nothing? He's not exactly the most amorous swain I ever heard of. But his mother wants him to get married; now there's a woman I'd better keep away from. Far, far away!

'If you're sure,' she said finally, 'I think I'll have a shower and get cleaned up. It will only take me a minute. I have to work tonight.'

'Work? I thought you ran a ranch?'

'I do. But ranching doesn't pay as well as it once did, so I moonlight. I have a job in the city three nights a week.'

He chuckled again. The smile lit up his face, turning the maze of little wrinkles into an extremely attractive painting. Lord, look at that, she told herself. A man's man—maybe even a woman's man! Too bad I'm not in the market!

She grinned at her own temerity as she watched him stalk down the stairs and head up towards the well. He walked with such—grace. A woman could do a lot worse than him, she told herself as she hurried down the hall to the bathroom.

Water was the only plentiful thing in the house. Gran had always enjoyed a good hot soak, and so, although the rest of the homestead had grown old and deteriorated, the hot-water system still gave one hundred and ten per cent. Alison stripped, dropping her clothing where she stood as the water steamed and the tub gradually filled. Hair, she told herself. Some day soon I've got to cut my hair. Look at it today, loaded with dust and dirt, hanging down my back like a bunch of brown string! Ugh! And the rest of me isn't much better. Too much bosom, too much bottom. Gran, trying to encourage her, had always said her only trouble was that she was too short. She had all the appurtenances of a six-foot lady, piled on a five-foot-four-inch frame. Alison shook her head disgustedly, avoided the big wall mirror, and climbed into the tub.

Fifteen minutes was all she could allow. Reluctantly, she climbed out of the cooling water, washed her hair in the basin, dried herself with one of the big bath towels, and used it as a sarong to get back to her bedroom. Her hair was still wet, and there was no time left for the drying. She made a turban out of another towel, and then picked through her wardrobe for something attractive. There wasn't much. Gran's project used up all the cash the ranch engendered, and left hardly anything for clothes. But her blue shirtwaister wasn't *too* bad.

Moving more quickly now, Allie slipped into briefs and bra, and a half-slip. She would have loved to go bra-less, but she jiggled. Shrugging her shoulders, she stuck out her tongue at herself in the mirror, slid the shirt-waister down over her head, and buttoned it. Except for the turban, she looked—not at all unattractive, she thought. Not beautiful, but healthy, normal—perhaps pleasant might be the word?

There was a noise from down the hall. Not the move-ments of a big man, but the scattered sounds of children. Smiling in anticipation, Allie tugged her dress around in front, slid her feet into her most comfortable slippers, and raced down the hall.

Carmen Hernandez had just come in. A short bronze-skinned woman, a good inch shorter than Allie, she showed all the facets of a typical Guatemalan of Mayan stock. The big smile on her face displayed a prominent gold tooth. She was out of breath. Two little girls giggled at her feet, one about eighteen months old, the other perhaps four or five. They were chattering in Quiché, one of the dominant dialects of the Mayan tongue, with a few Spanish words injected here and there.

'Ah, *linda*,' Carmen said. 'I all out of breath am! We have a wonderful time in the city, and *El Médico* says the children are very well!'

'Good,' Alison said. 'Is there any news?'

'*Sí.* Pedro says rain tonight. A bad storm. It should be the time, no?'

'So soon?' Alison shook her head. This was the part that hurt. 'Well, all right. Can you and Pablo...?'

'No trouble,' Carmen reported. 'You go to the city as usual, we make the preparations.'

The two women smiled at each other, understanding. The children, no longer willing to be put off, abandoned

their station behind Carmen and threw themselves at
Alison. The three of them went down to the floor in a
heap of giggling enjoyment, as they tried to hold Allie
down and tickle her at the same time. And that was just
the moment that Steady Colson chose to walk in,
unannounced.

'Who you are?' Carmen asked belligerently as she
barred his entry. From her position, sitting up against
the leg of the kitchen-table, Alison tried to control her
giggling. The children, seeing the strange man, ducked
behind Allie and tried to hide under the table.

'It's all right, Carmen.' Still puffing, Allie struggled
to her feet. 'Mr Colson is our new neighbour. He just
bought the old Harrison place down the road. Mr
Colson, this is Carmen Hernandez, my housekeeper.'

'Cuidado, linda,' Carmen said under her breath. *Este
hombre es muy peligroso! Tenga cuidado!'*

'Lovely language, Spanish.' That big grin was back
on Colson's face as he moved forward. Carmen stepped
aside, summoning the children with a flick of her wrist.
They dashed to her side and hid behind the swelling of
her bright red skirt.

'You speak Spanish?' Alison had both hands behind
her back, with crossed fingers on each. There had to be
some advantage that they could hold over his head.

'Not all that well,' he answered. 'I left these parts years
ago. I could make out the *"Sí"* and *"tenga cuidado"*,
but that's about the limit of it. What's the trouble? "Be
careful" of what?'

'Nothing important. It's just something she heard
downtown in the Old City,' Allie said. Carmen, who was
standing behind him now, was making strange gestures
with one hand, running it up and down the front of her

blouse. Trying to be unobtrusive, Alison did the same for herself.

In the course of her little wrestling match with the children, more of her buttons were open than fastened. Embarrassed, she wheeled around and buttoned feverishly. He laughed. Well, at least it changed the subject, Allie told herself. Funny, ha-ha! I wonder if you'd laugh if it were your——!

'Come.' Carmen swept up her little brood and herded them towards the hall. 'We unpack, *linda*, while you talk with this Mr Colson, no?' All three of them were out of the kitchen before he could think of something to say.

'They live on the fast track?' he asked, grinning.

'Children,' she replied. 'Everything must be full speed. Wonderful children.'

'I could see that,' he said. 'It's true what Harriet said. You'd like to have some of your own, too, I'll bet.'

'It takes two to tango,' she returned. 'I don't like to talk about it.' Not to you, Mr Stedman Colson, with your loving little assistant prosecuting attorney. Not at all!

'Then we won't. Let's talk about the well. Or do you object to that, too?'

'No, I'm more than willing to talk about my well. It's a deep subject, and I don't know very much about it, Mr Colson.'

'Steady,' he amended. 'Call me Steady. Deep subject? Are you one of those women who live on puns?'

Allie shook her head. 'I try to avoid them, but— occasionally they get away from me. What about my well?'

'A fine well, Alison. Deep. Sweet-tasting water. The windmill's in a precarious position, but a couple of days' work would shore it up. As for the pipeline, you only have to be a couple of inches deep to keep out of the weather. They say that the average winter temperature in San Antonio is fifty-nine degrees Fahrenheit. Sixty-two yards six inches, your ditch has to be. A trench-digger could do that for you in two hours, including travel time.'

'I don't doubt it,' she said. 'But there's a problem. I can't afford one. I looked into that. Trucking it all the way out from San Antonio would break my budget. No, I can't afford it. But thank you, Mr Colson.'

'Steady,' he repeated. 'Call me Steady. I just happen to have a trench-digger down at my place. Wouldn't need to be trucked at all. I'll just have one of my people drive up here in the morning with it, and you can have your ditch by noon.'

'That sounds delightful.' Her shaking head denied her words. 'But you don't hear too well. I can't afford it. Not an hour, not five minutes.'

'Well, look at it from my side, lady. The machine's sitting in my barn doing nothing. I have hands sitting around on their butts until my herd comes in. And I have a neighbour who——' He stopped in mid-sentence, and his jaw fell. 'Damn,' he said. 'All of a sudden you've become one pretty lady! What happened?'

'You not only don't hear, but you're half-blind as well, Mr Colson—I mean—Steady. I am certainly *not* one pretty lady. And all I did was wash. Plain soap, plain water, and plain Jane——'

'I don't know about this Jane,' he interrupted. 'But you're not the same girl who was digging that canal out there!'

'Got it in one,' she said morosely. 'Same girl.'

'Boy, are you down on yourself,' he commented. 'I'm an expert in girl-watching. Many years of experience! Believe me, you look nice!'

'I still think you need glasses,' she snapped.

'Well, if that's the way it is, I'll go along with the gag. Plain Jane, huh? OK by me.'

For just one moment Alison felt angry. He didn't *have* to give up that easily, did he? Of course, it was only a foolish teasing, but it wouldn't have hurt him to carry on for another five minutes. And, for a moment, there was an incipient tear in her eye. He wasn't handsome, she wasn't pretty—but surely there might be a place for the two of them? The world was crowded with plain, ordinary people, and yet the race went on propagating itself! Why not her?

'Hey, did I say something to upset you?' He was close enough to touch, and his left index finger was doing just that, swiping at the minuscule tear rolling down her cheek. She flinched.

'No, it wasn't anything. I—must have gotten something in my eye.'

'Then it's settled. I'll have my machine up here by, say, nine o'clock. Right?'

'I—didn't realise we had settled anything.' She mustered up her dignity, threw back her shoulders, and gave him her best 'Lady of the Manor' look. It proved to be an abject failure in the face of that enormous grin.

'Sure we did. Neighbours do neighbourly things. Besides, if I didn't, and my mother heard about it, there would be hell to pay.'

'Now you're going to tell me you're afraid of your mother?' She shook her head in disbelief.

'Wait until you see my mother. Well, now, we have a deal. About nine o'clock?'

It wasn't worth the fight. Suddenly tired, Alison leaned back against the table. 'Yes, we have a deal.'

He moved over to her again, closer than she wanted to entertain. But there was no place to run. Trapped between the table, two chairs, and his bulking presence, she could do nothing but clench her fists and hold them up against her breasts. 'Every deal has to be sealed,' he half whispered.

'I—you want me to sign something?' Her heart was hurtling down some unknown road, leaving logic behind.

'Nope. Sealed with a kiss, that's my way.' He stooped down to her, his big head shutting off the light. Like a rabbit mesmerised by the hawk's descent, Alison Springer closed both her eyes and waited. The contact never came. Instead, an angry siren sounded in the dusty area in front of the house, and brakes squealed.

'What the——?' he muttered as he let her go and turned towards the door. Fists pounded against the solid oak door. A flashing red and blue light cast macabre shadows through the window. He stalked over to the door and opened it.

Deputy Sheriff Clarence Chase was one of the old school of rural policemen. Big—almost as big as Steady—with a belly that hung over his belt grotesquely, he believed in the bellow and the bloodhound, rather than the fingerprint and diplomacy.

'Here, now, Alison Springer!' he roared, and then gulped as he came face to face with Steady Colson. 'Who the hell are you?'

'I think the question is who the hell are *you*? Close the door before the flies get in.'

The deputy, expecting an easy day with a houseful of women, was so startled that he did just that. But the movement was enough to restore his bluster.

'I'm a deputy sheriff,' he blustered. 'An' what I've got here is a search warrant. You got any objections, Miss Alison?'

Steady Colson stepped forward again, obviously about to make an objection, but Alison waved him to a stop. 'No, I don't mind,' she said. 'Your brother-in-law granted the warrant, I suppose?'

'Legal all the same,' Chase growled. 'He's a district judge. Duly elected and sworn in.' He turned back to the door and yelled something to the three men waiting outside. 'And me, I think I'll just sit here a spell, so you don't take it in your mind to hide anything, Miss Alison.'

Allie waved him into a chair, praying that the old furniture would hold his weight. 'Could I offer you a cup of coffee?' she asked.

'Tryin' to bribe a law officer?'

'With a cup of coffee?' Steady Colson pulled out a chair opposite the deputy, turned it backwards, and straddled it. 'Is that all it takes to bribe you? A cup of coffee?'

'Don't give me no sass,' the deputy grunted. 'Citizens owe respect to law officers.'

'Yeah, they do,' Colson snapped. 'But you have to earn it. My name's Colson. Stedman Colson the Third.'

'The Third? There's more like you?' Chase pushed his baseball cap to the back of his head. 'Why don't you just sit tight, Stedman Colson the Third. Miss Alison and me, we've been through this routine a time or two. Or, better still, why don't you mosey down the pike and leave us alone?'

'Don't think I'd want to do that,' Steady Colson allowed. 'Seems to me that Miss Springer here needs a lawyer.'

'And you just happen to be one?' The deputy looked up in disgust. 'Think you can faze me with that kind of talk? A lawyer, indeed.'

'A lawyer, indeed!' Steady Colson chuckled as he pulled out his wallet and handed over a calling card. 'Ambulance chasing, false arrest, slander—I do them all. In fact, I specialise in slander suits. How much are you worth, Deputy? I'd hate to bring a judgment against you and find out you can't pay.'

'Is this guy on the level, Miss Alison?'

'You have his word for it.' Allie ducked her head to keep from showing the laughter. She had indeed sat through two or more of these insistent searches, and none of them had been pleasant. It did her heart good to see the shoe on the other foot. 'And I'm asking Mr Colson to represent me.'

'Steady,' he whispered as he nudged her.

'Steady to represent me,' she amended her statement.

'Well, we're gonna find it this time,' Deputy Chase insisted. 'I followed that damn——'

'Uh-uh. Watch your language. There's a lady present,' Colson said.

It looked for a moment as if Chase had swallowed his tongue. When he recovered, red in the face, he followed again slowly.

'Me and my men, we followed that—truck—all last night, and all this morning. We know you made contact.'

'You mean Carmen made contact with somebody?'

'You know she did,' the deputy continued. 'And we would have gotten him dead to rights, except when we went to arrest him we ran into a Quinceares Party on the street, and what with all the noise and bands and the like——'

'You just happened to lose your suspect?' Colson interrupted.

The deputy muttered something unprintable under his breath and sat back in his chair.

'What kind of a party was that, Alison?'

'A typical Chicano celebration,' she told him with a chuckle. 'It's to observe the fifteenth birthday of the neighbourhood girls. In the old Spanish culture that's considered to be the coming of age—for girls, of course. I can't imagine why the deputy would think that anything happened on purpose to obstruct him.'

'Butter wouldn't melt in your mouth,' her lawyer whispered close to her ear.

'But it's all true,' she insisted. She was about to embroider the story a little further, but at that moment the deputy's helpers came into the room, pushing Carmen and the children in front of them.

'Ah, you found it?' Deputy Chase hauled himself up to his feet with a happy look on his face.

'Didn't find a thing. Nothin' but this——'

'Lady,' Colson interjected. 'This lady. Get your hands off her.'

The deputy heaved a huge sigh that shook his belly like a bowl of jelly. 'She's got herself a lawyer,' he announced.

'If you want to see Carmen's papers, I have them in my desk in the living-room,' Alison said. 'An American citizen, by marriage to a native-born citizen, and her two children—also American citizens. Shall I get them for you?'

The deputy waved his hand dispiritedly. 'No need. I seen them a half-dozen times before. And, you men, you didn't find nothin'?'

'How could we? We didn't know what we were looking for!'

'Oh—hell,' the deputy said. 'Get out of here. Go climb in the car.' He waited just long enough for the front door to slam behind them, then he turned around to Alison.

'Look, Miss Alison. I know you, and I knew your Gran before you. It don't do any good, all this carryin' on. I know you're smugglin', and you know you're smugglin'. So why don't you, just to save us time and the county's money—why don't you tell me what the hell you're smuggling?'

'Me? Smuggling?' It came out as a little squeak of alarm.

'My client denies this baseless charge,' Steady Colson said in his best baritone. 'And tomorrow I'll have a word with the judge who issued that stupid search warrant. In the meantime, Deputy, why don't you just haul your— get yourself off this spread? Miss Allie Springer is *not* in the smuggling business.'

Deputy Chase took one look at the anger displayed on Colson's face, started to say something, changed his mind, and stomped out of the house. In a moment the siren sounded and the county police car went out of the yard in a cloud of dust.

Steady Colson, displaying that big grin, came back over to Alison. She was breathless. Encounters like these were too much for her sensitive soul. She endured them, outwardly calm, but inwardly she was quivering like a leaf in the autumn wind. And she would feel that way all night, she knew.

'My client isn't, is she?' he asked. 'A smuggler?' Allie was astonished to find herself pinned against the table again. She struggled to work out a suitable answer.

'Now, where was I?' he mused. That big head bent over her; she closed her eyes in panic, and both her hands fastened in the cloth of his shirt, where it stretched tight over his shoulder muscles. This time there was no policeman, but she heard the sirens, the trumpets, and felt the lightning flashes as his warm, moist lips closed on hers.

Strangely enough, she dreamed of him all the rest of the afternoon.

CHAPTER TWO

THE house had settled down by four that afternoon. A small wind stirred the dust; little eddies climbed skywards, miniature tornadoes. Pablo came back from the hills, along with his two sheepdogs, Michael's grandchildren. He was a big man—for an Indian. Heavily muscled, bronze face, a constant smile, and a love for children that framed his life. He was a second-generation settler.

'I left the flock in Charbor canyon,' he reported as he swept off his ten-gallon hat and used it to beat the dust from his chaps. 'Plenty of water, the grass is high, and with that narrow box opening I don't think they'll stray. But there's always a chance of a mountain lion, Miss Alison.'

'I know.' She waved off his concerns. 'We've more important things to do, Pablo. Besides, we have new neighbours—suspicious neighbours. I wouldn't want them to find the flock straying.'

'Wouldn't do much for our reputation as shepherds,' he said with a chuckle. 'How did you ever get to be so—scheming?'

'It wasn't easy, Pablo. Now you'd better go check in with Carmen while I get dressed for the performance.'

'On the boats again? You sing?'

'Better believe it,' she said. 'Sing, dance, wait tables—anything to make a buck, Pablo. We're skinning things a little short lately.'

'My fault,' he replied. 'I should have taken more care in the lambing season. Lamb we can sell, mutton is just not the American way, hey?'

'Get out of here.' She sent him off with a pat on his shoulder and a big, shared grin. It was a local joke. Her grandparents had been German immigrants; his had been Guatemalan farmers. They represented a small minority in a sea of Mexicans—all American citizens.

She needed another shower. The interview with the deputy sheriff had exhausted her. Not that the ninety-degree August temperature wasn't helping! Bexar County, which included San Antonio itself, climbed down the side of the Balcone Escarpment. At its north-western corner it reached for the high ground of the Edwards Plateau. San Antonio was seven hundred feet above sea-level. From there the Lone Star state sloped downwards to the cluttered waterways of the Gulf Coast.

The Springer ranch was backed up against the escarpment, where drought and erosion had cut deep gullies in the land. Four miles down the road, in the lush bottom lands where the Medina River turned from a trickle to a creek, the Harrison spread was a cattleman's delight. But I won't have that many acres to worry about, Alison told herself as she showered, if I keep bringing it into the homestead in my hair!

With that as a warning, she ducked her head under the hot water again, and scrubbed mercilessly. It paid off. An hour later, still under the blow-drier, she noticed that the dusty brown had turned more red. Russet, perhaps, was a better term. It hardly matched her jet-black eyelashes, but a little skill with her make-up kit restored the balance. It would be a hot, humid night in town—providing the rains held off. She slipped into a lightweight set of cotton briefs, with a bra to match, and then into her flouncy Spanish gown. The light blue colour framed her long hair to perfection. The *décolletage* was a trifle deep for her own comfort, but Pedro loved it, and he was the boss of the performing team. The bodice clung to her voluptuous figure, and then the skirt flared out in a multitude of folds stretching down to mid-calf. Dozens of sequins drew patterns in which the candles could reflect. The shoes that matched had three-inch stiletto heels. Her sparkling hair, braided and formed into two wheel-cloches, one on either side of her head, was pinned up by two Spanish tortoiseshell combs. On the whole, she told herself as she made a last critical examination in her mirror, Cinderella has changed into the fairy princess quite nicely, thank you!

Carmen and the children agreed. They were all at the supper table in the kitchen when she came down. *'La magnífica!'* Carmen bobbed her head like a sparrow pecking at seed. Both the little girls climbed down from their chairs and ran towards Allie, but a stern command halted them. 'Jam,' Carmen explained. 'They eat jam all over they face and hands, no? Before you know, is all over you dress. *Vaya con Dios, linda.*

But Allie was not about to let the occasion pass. She snatched a wash cloth from the sink, made a vague pass at each of the girls, and then hugged them gently, without regard for the jam. There were tears in her eyes as she went out on to the veranda, a child escorting her on either side. But, of course, the children could not know. Sadly, she covered her hair with a black lace mantilla, and went out to the truck.

The Paseo del Rio—the River Walk—was a huge U-shaped diversion of the San Antonio river, including inside its bend several city blocks. It lay below the level of the streets, so that a person wandering its tree-lined walks or riding its barges would not be aware they were in the centre of one of the largest cities in Texas. Originally planned as a sewer project, it had quickly turned into a recreation area, filled with a maze of shops and restaurants and theatres. The barge grandly titled *Ciudad Mexico* was a flat-bottomed craft some forty feet long. Every inch of deck was crammed with tables. Aft, a small housing gave access to engines and steering. Since all cooking was done ashore, it was not *quite* a floating restaurant—but it was close enough to avoid a quibble.

Parking was always a problem. Alison found a space over at the Military Plaza, and walked up Commerce Street to join the boat at its temporary mooring just beyond the Aztec Theatre.

'Good,' Pedro said as she walked up the gangplank. 'Big crowd. Lawyers. Would you believe, lawyers?' Pedro's appreciation of the legal trade matched Shakespeare's.

'So they'll eat fast and talk a lot,' Alison declared as she checked herself out. There *was* a smear of strawberry jam on her skirt. Oh, well, it was worth it. 'Pedro, can we talk first, before they come aboard?'

'*Por qué no?* Why not? Best idea you ever had, Allie. Hold all our board meetings in public view. Who could suspect?' He waved his arm in a circular gathering movement, and the members of the mariachi band gathered around. Not a large band; four women, three men. Two guitars, two trumpets, one set of handdrums—and gourds to be shaken by those who conspired but had not the musical talent!

Pedro played first trumpet. He was young, barely twenty-six, the one Alison counted on for all the physical endeavours. His mother, Maria Santoso, played guitar and provided the shrewd judgement. 'I have word from Arturo,' she announced. 'He writes that six more packages must be moved in the next three months. Pressure is increasing. Here also,' Maria continued. 'We must be prepared for trouble. That new county attorney—she is like a tiger, that one. Already we have closed two way-stations, the——'

'No, don't tell us, Maria.' Alison looked at all of them. Night was falling. A waitress was lighting the shielded candles on each of the tables, and a babble of voices was approaching along the lighted River Walk at their stern. 'The fewer of us to know where the stations are, the less chance we'll leak the information. But I think we must—clear all the present goods. Every station, and then we can tell Arturo to send the rest, all at once.'

'After that,' Maria said with a sigh, 'it is perhaps time for us to shut down for a while. Pull in the heads, no?'

'I *hate* to do that,' Alison said fiercely.

'But, as they say, he who fights and runs away——'

'I know,' Alison said. 'Lives to fight another day. Vote of hands? Approved.' With a flutter of hands and a tuning of instruments the conspiracy council dissolved and instantly became a dance-band.

The entire barge had been leased for that one night for the San Antonio Bar Association's semi-annual dinner. When the last dinner-jacket-clad lawyer and his dinner-gowned accomplice came down the gangplank the inboard engine barked a couple of times, the lines were cast off, and the barge moved slowly down-river, just one in a procession of similar barges that would circle the Paseo, fighting for right of way. Alison and the rest of the women hurried through the crowd dispensing drinks, while the men played one or two light tunes.

Conversation was general. There was a breeze on the river, not only cooling, but keeping the insects at bay.

Hands busy and head down, Alison was up in the square bow of the barge before she noticed. Stedman Colson and Harriet Glebe were sitting at a table crowded with functionaries, she carrying on an animated lecture about one of her cases. He looks so different from the way he was this afternoon, Allie told herself. So polished! So distinguished. And something she hadn't noticed in the afternoon sun. Two little sprigs of white hair, one on either side of his head, just above his ears. Oh, wow, she giggled to herself, breaking the first rule of table-waiting: *always know where you are!*

There was barely room to wiggle sideways between the tables. Intent on her inspection, Alison, her tray loaded with drinks, had come an inch too close, bouncing off Harriet Glebe's shoulder and sending the blonde's hand and the Bloody Mary it held into convulsions.

'Oh, hell!' Harriet roared in anguish as she tried to push her chair back. Alison, too late to the fray, set her tray down and dabbed ineffectually at the rapidly spreading red mess. 'Get away from me!' Harriet yelled.

'I'm only trying to help,' Alison returned through gritted teeth.

'She's only trying to help.' Steady Colson's deep baritone voice, as he soothed his companion, took the towel out of Alison's hands, and put a quick end to the threat. 'There, now, everything's under control. I'm sure the management will replace your drink.'

'I'm sure they will.' Alison glared at him.

'Clumsy!' Harriet said without looking up. 'This town is full of incompetents. First that muddy little grub out at your ranch, and now this one!'

'It would be funny if they turned out to be the same girl,' Steady said. His smile revealed that he knew it to be true. He put one comforting arm round Harriet's shoulder and waved Alison away with the other. She went willingly. Harriet Glebe was still ranting at him about the calibre of labour in Bexar County.

'Almost lost a customer?' Pedro had put down his trumpet and was serving at the bar.

'A Bloody Mary,' Alison ordered. 'Maybe somebody else ought to take it. I'm mad enough to pour it over her head!'

'Treat them carefully,' Pedro advised. 'That one is the county attorney that's giving crime a headache. Glebe, the name is. Harriet Glebe.'

'I know her name.' Alison slammed her tray down on the improvised bar top. 'But the man with her?'

'That big one?' Maria had come over to join them. 'His name is Trouble, *linda*. With a capital T, no? You don't read in the papers about that flamboyant lawyer from California? The one who thinks he is Robins Hod?'

'Robin Hood,' Alison corrected gently. 'The trouble-maker? What's he doing here?'

'His mama, she come from around here,' Maria continued. 'She don't like life in Los Angeles. Too many gangs and shoot-em-ups. So he is like a good son, and he buys a place in Texas for her. You hear that, Pedro? Good to his mama, he is! Such a good son! Maybe he marries that woman, and makes her more—how do you say—*dulce*?'

'Sweet, Mama. Everybody is sweet to *you*,' Pedro said, laughing. 'But now we get the food out, and then a little music.' He picked up his trumpet and sounded a four-note call. The band members coalesced by the bar, and began playing.

Swaying to the soft beat, Allie picked up the microphone nervously, her fingers damp with perspiration. Not because of the crowd, she told herself. I've sung this song a hundred times before, to larger audiences. Then what? Because I don't want to *hear* people say *he* might marry *her*? Dear lord, he means nothing to me! Nothing! She had missed her introduction twice already. Pedro vamped them back into the lead-in one more time. With all the lonely passion that her throbbing contralto could muster, she sang the words to *Las Palomas*.

Some of the diners actually stopped eating to listen. There was even a smattering of applause. 'Hey, you don't sing that good before,' Pedro said in a quick aside before leading the group into *La Cucuracha*.

'No, I certainly don't,' she managed in a wry retort as she went back to the serving line. All the way across the barge she could see Steady Colson. He had stopped talking long enough to catch Allie's eye, and now he waved an approval. Her heart jumped just the slightest, and a little smile curled her lips and put a sparkle in her huge green eyes.

She sang three times more. The old Spanish love songs, full of sadness and longing: *Noche Triste, Cielito Lindo, Canción de Amor*. And finally, as the evening wore down, and black clouds started to scud across the summer moon, someone in the crowd who knew the routine shouted, 'The Hat Dance!'

Pedro looked enquiringly at her. It had been a long day, and Alison was bone-tired. Still, the crowd had come to be entertained. With a wry nod she slipped off her spiked shoes and fumbled around for the old pair of dancing flats that she kept aboard. The sturdy table that had been the food-service point, and then the bar, and before they docked would become the souvenir desk, was swept clean. Someone tossed a Mexican sombrero on to it, skidding it out to the middle. Two other pairs of hands swept under Allie's armpits and catapulted her to the table-top. The trumpets swept into the triumphant introduction, almost like a summons to the bullring, and Alison Springer, American-German-French girl of Texas, became a Spanish *doña*, dancing for her love.

The applause this time was tumultuous, as the lawyers came to their feet, followed reluctantly by their ladies. And then it was over. The barge nosed its way into the mooring, the gangplank was set, the customers hurried away to avoid the threatening rain. And he left without a word, Alison mourned to herself. What's Hecuba to him? She joined in the clean-up and then wearily made her way back down to the Military Plaza and her truck.

The rain was good to her. It held off until just after she slammed the truck door behind her. But then it came in a flood. She sat quietly in the cab of the truck, waiting for a break. A crazy place, this Texas, she mused. Seven years of drought. Seven long years. And then rains to follow, in cloudbursts. Those places that still had their grass cover absorbed the new rains, nourished themselves, and nurtured. Those which had lost their ground cover were gouged by the floods, their topsoil swept downstream, leaving them worse off than before. Alison shrugged. Her spread had been one of the losers. She pumped the accelerator, turned on her key, and the truck started.

The trip out of San Pedro Avenue was slow, rain-washed. The night-lights of the city sparkled on all sides, and there was a warmth and a freshness to the falling water. She cracked open the driver's window and inhaled the magnificence of it all. There was little competing traffic as the straight-as-a-die avenue swept past the bedroom communities: Laurel Heights, Los Angeles Heights, Shearer Hills, Dellwood Park, and then out to the Military Drive, the long loop that engirdled the city. Beyond the loop the country began. She shifted to State Route 2696, branched off at last on to the Farm-to-Market Road going westward, and turned at last on to the narrow, winding way, only partly paved, that led by the Harrison spread—I suppose I should learn to call it the Colson spread, she thought—and then she was home.

The old farmhouse, hidden in the shadow of its plane trees, was as dark as the night. The little Volkswagen camper was at the front door, its engine turning over, its lights barely seen under the curtain of rain. Alison pulled up alongside and climbed out.

'Everything all right?' She came up on Carmen's side of the camper.

'Everything OK, *linda*. You have a good night?'

'Lots of applause, not much tipping,' Alison replied. 'Be very careful. The roads are slick. Don't take any chances!'

'My Pablo, he takes care of everything,' Carmen said. She reached over in the darkness and patted the driver's hand.

'See that?' Pablo contributed. 'Alison, when you find a man that you think about *that* way, marry him!' He laughed raucously.

'Shush,' Carmen chided.

'When I feel that way about some man, I'll take two aspirin and go to bed,' Alison said. 'Alone! *Vaya con Dios!*' She stepped back. The little van began to move out into the storm. Affectionately, Alison patted the back of the vehicle as it glided out into the dark of night. They would be gone twenty-four hours, if everything went well.

It was worth a small prayer as she prepared for bed. There were so many things that *could* go wrong. But the game was something she *had* to play. The idea had come to her during her year in Guatemala with the Peace Corps. Gran had approved enthusiastically, helping her to set up the couriers, the organisation, the way-stations. And I am *not* going to let it all be threatened by some overgrown goon who's moved in down the road, she thought defiantly as she pulled the sheets up to her chin and composed herself.

It was almost a pleasure to be awakened by the noise. Alison had spent the night tossing and turning. For some stupid reason, the face of her new neighbour kept popping up on the inside of her eyelids. Stedman Colson, leaning close, kissing her. Stedman Colson, dressed in judicial robes, shouting from the Bench, 'Guilty! Ten thousand years in jail! Take her away!' Stedman Colson, shaking his finger just under her nose, saying 'Naughty, naughty!' Stedman Colson, standing in the doorway of the First Methodist Church, waving goodbye to her before he turned to go down the aisle towards Harriet Glebe.

It was that last that so exasperated her. She kicked the sheets off and put one foot on the floor—and then heard the noise. Or maybe it was the other way around? In any event, with only one eye open, dressed in the little cotton shorty nightgown that she favoured, she fumbled her way to the window, looked out—and groaned. Stedman Colson sat casually in the saddle of a complicated ditch-digging machine nestled close against the house, looking over his shoulder at a very neat sixty feet of ploughed earth! And then he turned and looked squarely at her through the window, and grinned.

'Dear lord,' she muttered as she dropped the corner of the dimity curtain and backed away. Even the sheriff would have been a more welcome sight than he. And he would undoubtedly want to come in and be rewarded for his—nightgown! Reason made an attempt to overcome her gibbering mind. Nightgown! *Whatever else might happen, he must not see me in this excuse for a nightgown!* In the fastest quick-change ever known to the female of the species, she translated herself into trousers, socks, a blouse, and her flat red sneakers, and went dashing for the front door. The machine was shut off, huddling against the northwest side of the building. Mr Stedman 'Call me Steady' Colson was sitting on the front stoop, nibbling on a stack of long fescue grass.

'I thank you very much,' she offered with extreme formality. He was up on his feet in an instant, that big grin still plastered on his face.

'No trouble at all. Not for neighbours.' He pushed his hat back. Alison had the strange suspicion that he was laughing at her.

'Terribly early for that sort of work,' she stated cautiously.

'Mustn't waste a minute of this beautiful sunshine,' he said. 'See you was out late last night?'

She waved a hand vaguely. 'All in a day's work.'

He stared at her. It was like a ritual courting dance, and, being a Texas woman, she knew just what was expected, but offered it with a certain lack of enthusiasm. 'Then you couldn't have had breakfast. Won't you come in and join me?'

'Don't mind if I do.' He brushed himself off, scraped his shoes on the mat in front of the door, and followed her. Altogether too well-trained, she told herself grimly as she led the way into the kitchen. And why——?

'And why do you keep talking like some cowpoke?' She put it in words rather than let the suspicion hang.

'Because that's what I am,' he replied, chuckling.

'You're a lawyer!' A firm declaration, just to let him know she had been——

'Checking up on me?' he interrupted her thought.

'Well, a man of your reputation, who just suddenly appears out in the back lots, you know. And then begins to imitate the locals—if that's what you're doing. And goes dining on the Paseo—lord, those prices are high.'

'And how would you know that, little lady?'

'Because I'm the one who sets the prices on our boat!' she snapped. 'Sit down. No, not on that——'

The warning was just a second too late. He had lowered his bulk into the most fragile chair in the kitchen, and it collapsed under his weight. But he did not fall with it; with effortless ease he caught himself, stretched, and was up again, still grinning.

'I'm sorry,' she apologised. 'It's been so long since we've had anyone as big as—I mean, the chair needed mending, and——'

'I know what you mean,' he said. 'How about this one? I weigh in at one hundred ninety-five. Too fat for your furniture?'

'I—didn't mean anything like that, honestly.' She moved around him like a roper checking a horse, nervously. 'Try this one. And I don't think you're fat. I don't see an ounce of fat...' Her voice faltered to a stop. He wasn't showing fat, but he was showing almost everything else. Dressed only in a pair of ragged khaki shorts, his muscles gleaming with perspiration, he looked like some Athenian movie hero. She blinked her eyes a couple of times and swallowed hard.

'Would you want to shower—or something?'

'Suppose I just stick my head under the kitchen tap?' he asked, and then went to do just that, as if she had agreed. In truth, her tongue was stalled in neutral; she couldn't have answered him if her life had depended on it. For one anxious moment she watched as he bent over and ducked under the water-flow. Move, her mind shouted at her. Move, before he turns around and bites you!

She moved. There was a flash of rebellion as she did so. It might have been nice to be bitten, her subconscious mind insisted. But she was moving. Over to the butane gas stove, to put the coffee to boiling. Back to the refrigerator for eggs and ham, and then a struggle to remember where the skillet had ended up. And by this time she had recovered her equilibrium, and he had come up for breath, spluttering.

'There's a towel on the rack to your right,' she called over to him, refusing to come a step nearer. Somehow or another she got the eggs into the skillet before the butter, but no catastrophe resulted. The bread slices didn't seem to fit the toaster, but the ham was browning nicely, and there were a few left-over potatoes that could be pan-fried, and that ought to please him. Get a hold on yourself, she commanded. Don't dither. He's only a man; nice-looking, but only a man. And one who could do us a heap of harm. Don't pamper him; he'll want to come back again some day!

Which explained why, when he came back and sat down, the situation had reversed. The cold food had become warm; his hostess had become cool. Perhaps even downright chilly.

'I really can't afford to pay you for the work, Mr Colson,' she said. 'Besides, I thought you were going to send one of your hands down to do the work?'

'Matter of semantics,' he said around the corners of a mouthful of food. 'I couldn't send one hand down without the other. They come in pairs.'

'Heaven preserve me from people who make puns at breakfast,' she sighed.

'You're not an early-morning person, are you?' He had stopped to sip the coffee, and his nose wrinkled.

'No, I'm not. And I hate cheerful people before noontime.' She didn't *want* to sound grumpy, it just came out that way. And, besides, it was absolutely true. 'Is something wrong with the coffee?'

'Could be a mite stronger,' he allowed. 'I'm glad I came. I'm finding out lots about you that I would never have known! Wish I had brought my notebook, but maybe I can remember it well enough to get it written down.'

'What in the world are you talking about?' she asked. 'I know they raise people differently in California, but— why would you want to write everything down about me?' The suspicion had come too late, she recognised. Of course lawyers wrote everything down. But wasn't there supposed to be some warning first? Or was that just sheriffs? She glued both her lips together in one grim line, and defied him to get another word out of her.

'Well,' he drawled, 'I'm fixin' to forget everything I learned in California. Got me a good spread now, my maw's happier than a clam at high tide, and I aim to set myself up in the cattle business.'

'That's just too much,' she said disgustedly, forgetting her resolve. 'Not even a Texas cowpoke talks that way any more. You sound like a bad movie.'

'Gave myself away, did I?' That big grin was back. It was almost impossible to be angry with such a personality.

'It was that business about the clam at high tide,' she admonished. 'You have to be all the way down at Houston before you run into a clam. Or high tide, for that matter. Now just why *did* you come over this morning, Mr Colson?'

'Steady,' he insisted. 'Only my accountant calls me Mr Colson, and that only on April fifteenth.'

'All right, Steady,' she replied. 'Now—why?'

'Oh, a dozen things. By the way, this is mighty good food. Gives a fellow a sense of cheer when he finds a woman who can cook.'

'Nonsense. It's only breakfast. Any fool can make breakfast. I've even known some men who could cook breakfast without poisoning themselves. What about Miss Glebe? I'll bet she can cook up a storm.'

'Not exactly. I doubt if Miss Glebe could boil water without burning it. She's one great prosecutor, but householding is not her style.'

Alison glared at him. So, if he planned to marry Harriet Glebe, maybe he was thinking of hiring a cook? Could that be what this was all about? It hardly seemed possible. Much more possible was the idea that he had taken the sheriff's complaint to heart, and was nosing around to set up a trap for her! Well, it would be a long, cold day in Dallas before he got away with it.

'So where's all the kids?' His question, hard on her suspicions, sent her into a tailspin. He *was* snooping, and she had to think of a quick answer.

'Oh, they went into town with their parents,' she said. 'It's a Chicano holiday down in *La Villita*, the old Spanish *barrio* in the centre of town. Some saint's day.' Which wasn't a bad suggestion. There were more saint's days celebrated down in the *barrio* than anyone could

shake a stick at! 'And the mayor is giving a speech.'
Another certainty.

'Two cute little kids,' he commented as he wiped his
plate clean. 'Well, now, that relieves my stomach and
my mother's mind at the same time. She'll be fussing
about my going off without breakfast. But I must be on
my way. Singing on the River tonight, are you?'

'Tomorrow night,' she said. 'We do it three times a
week.'

'Mighty fine entertainment,' he said as he stood up.
'Told my mother all about it. She was real taken, having
a neighbour who digs ditches and sings and dances.
Wouldn't be surprised if she didn't wander up to see you
one of these days. Now, about the pipe?'

'Pipe?'

'Pipe,' he said patiently. 'You know. The pipe you
put in the ditch to carry the water down to the house
and make everything all peachy clean?'

'Oh, that.' She shook her head and sighed. 'That has
to wait, Steady. We just don't have the money right now
for piping. *Poco a poco*, a little at a time, that's the way
we have to do things on this spread.'

'Sounds like a good idea,' he returned. '*Poco a poco*.
I must remember that phrase. Now, do we shake hands,
or do I get to kiss you?'

'Oh, lord, no!' She put both hands up in front of her
protectively, and backed away as he slowly stalked her
across the kitchen. It was a roomy workplace, but
eventually her back came up against the sink, his arms
came down, one on either side of her, and she was
trapped.

'Oh, no, what?' he asked, his voice barely a whisper.
'No kiss, or no handshake?'

'No,' she stuttered. 'Just—I—no kissing.'

'Is there some reason for that, or do you just not like men?'

Both her hands were up against his chest, pushing, but there was no give to the man. She was shaken, but wanted him to know why, and finding the words was difficult.

'No—kissing,' she repeated. 'I—yes, we could shake hands. No, I like *some* men.' Yes, I like kissing, she wanted to say. Yes, I like kissing *you* very much. But I'm not going to. I'm afraid. Not of you, but of myself. I'm afraid that I might like it too much, and you're already engaged to Harriet Glebe. And I'm afraid that you've come to poke and pry into my business, and that I can't allow. Not at all!

When she looked up from lowered eyes he was grinning again. 'So what it amounts to is that you just don't like *me* enough,' he said solemnly. 'Well, it's not something you can force on a girl when you've just met her. So I'll just have to try harder, won't I?'

'Why would you want to?' It was a question whose answer she wanted desperately, which made it difficult to word the thing casually.

'Why would I want to?' He pursed his lips and that gleam was back in his eye. 'Because I like you? Because you're a beautiful little thing when you get all cleaned up? Because I admire women with guts and determination? Because my mother wants me to get married and raise grandchildren? Oh, there must be a dozen more reasons—but that ought to be enough to start on.' He stepped away, stuck out his hand, and grinned.

Damn that grin, she told herself as she hesitantly wiped her hand on her trousers and watched in amazement as it was swallowed up in his mammoth paw. It's the grin that throws me off balance, and he knows it! But, like a sweet little child after her lessons, she said, 'Thank you again, Mr Colson. I hope I will see more of you.'

He looked down at his tattered shorts, and that grin, if possible, became even bigger. 'Not hardly possible, ma'am,' he drawled. 'Not without revealing *all* the family secrets. But, yes, I hope to see a great deal more of you, Alison Springer.'

And with that and a tip of his hat, he clattered out of the front door and over to his machine. Alison took a couple of hesitant steps after him, but froze at the door. He was back in the saddle of his little machine; it started at the turn of the key, and the pair of them went waddling down towards the road and out of sight.

And what was that all about? Alison asked herself after he had gone. Just a friendly visit? 'I hope to see a great deal more of you, Alison Springer'? Just neighbour-talk, or was there something suggestive about the whole conversation? 'My mother wants me to get married'? Good lord, nobody is *that* good to their mother these days! Nobody. But what if——?

With a little scream of frustration she snatched her hat down off the peg by the front door, pulled it down over her mass of russet hair, and headed down and around the hill towards the barn. With Pablo gone, someone else had to exercise the two saddle horses and feed them, and check on Killer, the famous rodeo horse, who brought in just a little more income to the embattled homestead.

CHAPTER THREE

THE afternoon passed as in a dream. The warm weather held. Life seemed to slow down in South Texas. Even the birds abandoned the skies and roosted in what shade they could find. After her burst of enthusiasm with the horses, and a quick check on the sheep, Alison came back to the old homestead, showered, and went out to the porch. Michael was her only company. She had taken the younger dogs with her up into the mountains, and left them there with strict orders to guard the flock. But Michael was too old for that. He had been Gran Springer's dog; the skills were all there, but the flesh was weak. Now, as Alison stretched out on the porch swing, he lay down beside her, his head between his paws.

'Lovely day for napping, Michael.' Her right hand hung over the edge of the swing, close enough to scratch the dog's neck. The animal wheezed his appreciation. Alison closed her eyes and let her lively imagination run free.

Faces danced before her. Dan Springer, her father, the original unlucky man. Through years of an earlier drought he had nursed his tiny two hundred acres, making enough to feed himself and his daughter. And then the rains came, the Nueces River burst into flood, and poor Dan Springer was drowned in the spring freshet. Fifteen years ago, and eleven-year-old Alison had come to live with her Gran.

Her eyes were wet; a memorial for Dan Springer? Or for his lonely daughter, caught up in what she considered to be her duties? But lonely, none the less. Not since she had graduated from nursing school had she been with friends. Oh, the members of her council were friends—but most of them were twice her age. She lived so far out of town, and was so eternally busy, that there hadn't been any 'young men'. Or even middle-aged ones, for that matter. Which was one reason why she did love to tease Deputy Sheriff Chase. At least he was a man. The dog stirred under her hand, and managed a very weak 'wuff'. Alison managed to open one eye.

In the world of small people, Alison was no giant. But the little old lady who stood on the bottom step of the veranda could be best classified as 'tiny'.

'I really didn't mean to wake you up.' A soft, husky voice from a heart-shaped face. Tanned skin, blue eyes, pure-white hair. Not an inch of extra flesh; she looked as if she might weigh eighty pounds, and be threatened by strong winds. Her right hand rested on a curiously carved mahogany cane. Behind her a gleaming two-wheeled gig stood, the pony in harness doing its best to nuzzle nourishment from the widespread clumps of grass. 'I'm your new neighbour.'

Alison snapped to attention, swinging both feet to the floor. Her hand went almost unconsciously to her hair, but there was nothing that could be done to the mess. This woman was *his* mother! She sprang to her feet and moved to the edge of the veranda. 'I'm Alison Springer,' she said, offering a hand. The little lady smiled and climbed the remaining steps.

'Abigail Colson,' she said. 'You don't hear that name very much these days—Abigail—but it was once a favourite, at least up in Oklahoma.'

Alison gestured towards the old rocking-chair stuffed with cushions. Mrs Colson sank into them with an audible sigh of relief. 'I don't know if that fool pony will stand.'

'I'll call Pablo and—oh, lord, Pablo's not home.' Her face turned several shades of rose before settling down again. 'Let me take him around to the side. There's shade and water, and I'll be right back.'

'Don't hurry on my account,' Mrs Colson said, but Alison had already gone. By the time she came back, panting, Stedman's mother was rocking steadily and fanning herself.

'My gran's fan,' Alison explained. 'She always liked to sit here after the work was done and fan herself.' So why am I standing here twisting my fingers behind my back, as if she were the high school principal? She's only a neighbour, come to call! 'Could I get you some lemonade?'

A big smile spread over Mrs Colson's face. So that's where he gets it from, Allie thought! 'Lemonade and cookies? That's the way it used to be down home. Out in California it would be cocktails and gossip. Hate that place. I really do. But then, my son said you were the old-fashioned type.'

'Where in the world did he get *that* idea?' Alison gasped.

Those faded blue eyes sparkled at her. 'Did he get it wrong?' A gentle question, as if the answer were sure.

'I—guess, according to his lights, I am,' Allie admitted wistfully. 'He travels in the highest society, I suppose?'

'It all depends on your point of view,' the old lady said as she shifted to get herself comfortable. 'Fine old chair. Handmade?'

'Yes. By my grandfather. My gran swore it was the best chair in the world for thinking!'

'Best society,' Mrs Colson mused. 'There are some fine people in the best society—but not many. I've seen more good hearts in Selman, Oklahoma, than in Los Angeles, California. No, Steady's been travelling in fast society, not necessarily high society. And you?'

'I'd better get the lemonade,' Alison replied, evading the question. 'The weekly paper is there on the settle.' Mrs Colson waved her off.

'I'd rather look at the scenery,' she insisted. Alison jumped for the door.

Was it Murphy's law that said anything you want in a hurry can't be found? There wasn't any lemonade already made, she couldn't find the fresh lemons, and finally Alison was reduced to opening a can of frozen juice. But there were homemade chocolate chip cookies, and when she staggered out on to the porch with the big tray it was adorned in a manner that even Gran would have approved.

'Ah. Mighty good on a hot day.' Mrs Colson emptied her first glass in one long gulp, then helped herself to the pitcher. 'And cookies. Store-bought?'

'Made them myself,' Alison admitted, thinking, What is it about these Colsons? They've enough money to buy half the county, the way I hear it, and both of them are madly interested in the idea that I can cook! Good lord, is *that* the trap? He and his mother want to hire me to go for a cook at their spread? And if I'm asked, what in the world could I say?

'Good thing,' Mrs Colson reflected. 'A girl ought to be able to out-think a man any day, and still run a kitchen. Don't you agree?'

It was so close to what Gran Springer always allowed that Alison almost swallowed her tongue.

'I see that you do. That's nice. Run this whole spread by yourself, do you?'

'No.' Alison took a deep breath. Just sitting here listening had been as hard as running a mile barefoot! 'No. I have a Chicano couple who help, but they're away for the day.'

'Ah. That's where the children come in? My son was agog about those children.'

'We are, too,' Alison said. 'They're a fine pair—but terribly changeable, you know. One day they'll welcome strangers, and the next they're terrified.'

'Wonderful creatures, children,' Mrs Colson said. 'Meant to have a half-dozen myself, but only ended up with one. Man proposes, God disposes—isn't that out of the Good Book?'

Alison, whose Biblical education had been sadly neglected, nodded as if she were sure of the quote, and hoped there would be no further inquisition. It was a fruitless hope.

'Mean to have any of your own?' the old lady enquired. 'Children, I mean?'

'I—hadn't given it much thought,' Alison lied. Four had always been her ideal. But first, in the age-old custom, a girl had to catch a husband, right?

'Ought to think about it,' the old lady commented as she struggled to her feet. 'You're getting on, my dear. Best to have them when you're young, you know.'

'Do you have to go so soon, Mrs Colson?'

'Abigail. Call me Abigail, girl. Yes, I have to go almost at once. There are a million things to get done about the house. Men don't understand that.'

'I suppose not,' Alison replied. 'And I hear your son plans to get married soon?'

The old lady stopped, one hand on the rail, and turned to smile over her shoulder. 'Tell you that, did he? The bit about how his mother keeps pleading with him to get married? Biggest con-man this side of the Rio Grande, my son Stedman. Why would I want him to get married? He looks after me something marvellous. If he marries, there goes my little nest. And besides, I know him well. Why would I wish a man like that off on some unsuspecting girl? You must come and see me when you can. Bring the children.'

'Yes—I—yes.' The dog managed to get tangled under Allie's feet as she struggled down the stairs to bring the gig around. But for her dancer's skill she would have landed on her fundament. But at least the pony was ready to go. Mrs Colson needed an arm up, but once in the gig she was totally in control.

'Come and see me soon.' The command drifted down on the wind as the team circled the flat area in front of the house and headed for the road. Not until it drifted out of sight did Alison begin to breathe normally again.

As the afternoon waned Alison began to feel that strange excitement in her stomach that always accompanied the waiting hours. The clouds were coming in again, dark thunderheads against the eastern sky. It was as if heaven were judging her, and she shivered as she went into the dim kitchen and made herself a cup of tea and a sandwich.

It tasted like sawdust, that sandwich. As it always did. The minute hand on the old pendulum clock seemed to be stuck in place. She got up nervously and checked the movement with her finger, to no avail. Think of something else, she told herself fiercely.

Five o'clock passed. The wind was kicking up little spurts of movement among the plane trees that provided a windbreak for the house. Her great-grandfather had planted them just for that purpose. A loose shutter in the west wing began to bang. She ran to fasten it. By the time she came back her tea was cold. She shrugged her shoulders and prowled the empty house. Michael, still out on the porch, whined at her coming and going.

Six o'clock. The sky was so dark that sunset had come early. The wind was up to twenty knots, and trees were bending before it. Wanting something to do, she took a lantern and went down to the barn. Her own mare whinnied at her; Pablo's big mustang stamped a hoof. Killer, segregated in a doubly strong padded stall, kicked at the boards to show his disgust, and then went silent. Behind the barn, the hens were roosting. In their little pen, the ducks huddled together. All the animals were waiting for the storm, and there was nothing a mere female could do to comfort them. Wearily Alison made her way back up the hill, the lantern swinging in her hand.

And she waited.

By ten o'clock her fingernails were down to the quick. The storm had brought thunder with it, strong enough to rock the old house, beating on her nerves. It didn't help to think that in the darkness the trucks could steal by Steady Colson's house, and not be noted. Nothing helped. Alison Springer was up to her neck with pressure, and about to bail out.

And then the truck came.

Up from the Gulf it came, not from the border. Rain-washed, driven by a taciturn Anglo who hardly spared two words.

'Both packages?' Alison asked.

'Both. Where do you want them?'

'In here.' Alison took one; he took the other, and followed her down to the disused east wing.

'Bad trip?' Alison laid her bundle down, he put his alongside.

'Bad enough. Gonna be a whopper, this one. I got to get back tonight.'

'I know. God bless.'

'As you say.' And he was gone. And why were we whispering? she asked herself. There's nobody within five miles, but we whisper like great conspirators. She giggled, relieving her own tensions. Very suddenly she felt tired. Worn to the bone. Nothing physical had done it; it was the terrible cycle. Tension and release, and then more tension, like the torture wheel of the inquisition.

Alison went back to the kitchen and did the unforgivable. She reheated her tea in the old pan on the back of the stove, winced at its taste, but drank it nevertheless. Things moved faster now. Carmen and Pablo would be along shortly—if all went well. And Pablo, being a man of huge appetites, would want something to dull the one in his stomach. Luckily he liked spaghetti. Alison whipped out the ingredients and began to work.

At twelve o'clock the little Volkswagen camper grumbled up outside the door, and in a moment Carmen and Pàblo came in, arm in arm. 'Everything went well,' Pablo announced in his booming voice. 'To the minute, mind you, didn't it, *amore*?'

'Yes. Like the clock,' Carmen agreed as she snuggled up against her husband and then, unaccountably, began to cry.

'Women!' Pablo said. 'Who can understand them?'

'I'm almost crying myself,' Alison retorted. 'The new packages are in. We have a lot to do.'

'I'll go look,' Carmen interjected.

'Your dinner's ready. It'll get cold,' Alison said. 'I made Italian.'

'We'll eat first, and *then* we'll go look,' Pablo decided. So, what with dinner, a long conversation about the trip, and considerable work with the new packages, it wasn't until two in the morning that they managed to get to sleep, leaving all the dirty dishes standing in the kitchen sink.

It wasn't exactly bluebirds making all that noise just after sunrise. Alison came awake with a jerk, worrying that the noise would awaken the children. Her ancient royal-blue robe was at hand. She shrugged herself into it and rushed to the front door, prepared to raise a ruckus. In fact, she had barely belted the robe closed as she stepped out on the porch and glared at the two trucks.

They were coming slowly down the line of the ditch that Steady Colson had dug for the water-pipes. Barely a day before? It hardly seemed possible. And now the two trucks, one after the other, and a pair of men throwing off lengths of pipe as they came slowly down the hill. George Two Feathers was driving the first truck. She knew him well. They had been schoolmates up until the tenth grade, when George had dropped out to go to work in his father's plumbing supply shop.

Alison raced down the stairs in her bare feet and went up the line about twenty paces, madly waving her hands. The trucks came to a stop, and George leaned out of the door.

'The children are still asleep,' she yelled at him. 'They need their rest!'

'Don't we all?' he replied. 'But I don't know any way to unload pipe quietly. You've growed to be a pretty girl, Alison!'

'Never mind the flattery,' she muttered as she climbed up on to the running board of the vehicle. 'And never mind the pipe. You must have made some mistake. I didn't order any pipe.'

George had never been the sharpest wit in the county, but he *was* thorough. He had to be. His had been an Oglala Sioux Indian family which left the reservation to follow the rodeo circuit, and had eventually settled in South Texas. Alison fumed as he leafed slowly through the orders on his clipboard.

'Nope. No mistake, Allie. Miss Alison Springer, Springer Ranch, RFD Route 627. Not hardly a doubt. Sixty yards of six-inch water-pipe, complete with joints and attachments. Right place, right goods, Allie. You gotta get out of the way so I can get on with the work.'

'George Two Feathers!' Allie snapped. 'Stop it this instant. I didn't order any water-pipe. I'd like to have it, but I couldn't pay for it if it came at two cents a running foot. Now pick up all that—pipe—and get out of here. And if you wake the babies I'll skin you six ways from Sunday!'

He grinned as he climbed down from the truck. At six foot four, he was a massive man, as fit as any long-ago warrior of his tribe had ever been. And he had a sense of humour. He looked down at the top of her head and shrugged his shoulders. 'OK, Allie, make me.'

'George,' she fumed. 'You men make me sick! Go ahead, leave it all to clutter up my yard! But I'm darned if I'll pay you a penny, you——'

'No call to get all excited,' he said solemnly. 'It's all paid for. And Harry Gibson is coming right behind us to connect and cover.'

'All paid for?' A new idea is always worth a cautious approach, thought Alison. Who in heaven would want to pay for *my* pipeline? 'Not that Colson fellow, was it?' she asked suspiciously. George looked down at the sheet.

'Nope. Some committee or somethin' in town.'

No, it can't be, she told herself. The only committee I'm familiar with, in town or out, couldn't muster postage for a complaint to the governor! But there isn't anyone else!

'What the trouble is?' Carmen called from the veranda, a child cuddled close in her arms. *'Linda?'*

'Oh—nothing. No trouble at all. Just a small mix-up. All right, George, go ahead. But if it all turns out to be a mistake, don't blame me, y'hear?'

'Oh, I hear.' The tall Indian man swung himself back up into the truck, waved to his mate, who was driving behind him, and the procession went on. Alison backed up out of the way, moving gradually until she was at Carmen's side.

'I know it's a problem, but I don't know what kind, or what to do about it.' Her voice was weary. Dependable old Alison is running out of gas, she told herself. Every little thing that goes wrong puts me in a tizzy. It never was this way before that darn Colson man wandered into the area.

The two trucks concluded their mission, George Two Feathers tooted his horn and waved at her, and they drove away, raising a cloud of dust. And that's another thing, she thought. Last night it rained enough to float the Titanic; this morning the yard is as dry as a bone again! If only we could get some grass to grow. Damn!'

'Pipes only a little problem,' Carmen said. 'Look, *linda*. Baby has trouble with the leg, no?'

Alison whirled around, all her previous complaints washed away. The tiny child clung to Carmen's neck and ducked her head away, too shy or too frightened to say anything. '*La derecha*—the right one,' Carmen said.

'To the doctor—at once,' Alison said.

'But—the money, the appointment? You know how they are at the hospital, no?'

'Damn the money,' Alison growled. 'Take her in now. I'll call Don Pancho. He owes us. Where's Pablo?'

'He give breakfast to Juanita. They are—what you say—A-OK.'

Alison tried to lighten the atmosphere. The little Guatemalan mother was almost in a state of panic. 'No, we never say anything like that. It was all made up, that A-OK business. Can you drive to the city?'

'*Seguro!*'

'Then—*vamos*. And—Carmen?'

'*Sí?*'

'Don't worry, love. That's my job, doing the worrying around here. Pablo and I, we'll take care of everything. *Vamos!*'

'*Me voy. Gracias a Dios por usted.*'

'And thank God for you, too,' Alison murmured. 'The van is down in the barn. Get ready. I'll bring it up to the door.'

She ran all the way, down the hill, around the curve and into the barn itself. The horses, startled, stamped and neighed. She ignored them all, starting up the little van and backing it out.

Up at the house again, she pulled up by the steps of the veranda just in time to meet a four-wheel-drive wagon coming in from the road. 'Trouble?' Steady Colson managed to squeeze his bulk out from behind the wheel and walk over to her.

Of all the things or people I need at just this moment, she thought, this is the farthest out! Like a hole in the head, I need *him*. I'd be better off if it were the deputy sheriff instead!

Just looking at him gave her nervous palpitations. Or was it just nerves? She pushed the idea aside as Carmen came down the stairs. This time the baby was wrapped in a blanket, with only her head on view.

'We have to get Conchita to the doctor's,' Alison explained. All her worry was in her voice, and he marked it.

'I'll drive. And we'll go in *my* car,' he said as he held the door open. Carmen hesitated, vacillating between Colson and Alison. 'For the baby,' she sighed.

In that instant, Alison's mind was made up. 'Of course. Go with him,' she said. 'I'll telephone ahead and make the arrangements. Call me as soon as you learn something, Carmen.'

'*Sí, senorita.*'

'And—thank you very much, Mr Colson.' It was a difficult thing to do, making her voice sound as calm and as casual as it would on a Sunday afternoon at a picnic.

'You bet,' he replied, and there was something different about his voice, too. As if he knew something, but wasn't aware of what he knew. He paused for a moment, the door of the car open, and then he slammed it shut, squeezed into the driver's seat, and gunned the engine. They were gone in a cloud of dust, moving like a scared coyote.

Pablo came out on the veranda with Juanita in his arms. The four-year-old was upset, but quiet. Alison offered to take the child, but the little girl withdrew. She had found her comfort in the man's trusting care. And that's something we have to overcome, Allie told herself.

'Shy,' Pablo said. 'And especially now that her sister is gone, Miss Allie. But I have to get to the sheep—and the chickens—and the pigs. You think that Mr Colson will make trouble?'

Alison, who had been day-dreaming about that very fellow, snapped herself out of it. 'Mr Colson? He's already making trouble,' she answered. 'Oh, you mean about the baby? I haven't any idea. Not a clue. Has she eaten?'

'Breakfast of a sort,' Pablo reported. 'Tortillas and milk. Some day, when we get enough money, we must buy a cow.'

'Put her down on the swing,' Alison instructed. 'I'll see what I can do. And don't worry about us—we'll get along, eventually.'

The big Chicano smiled at her. He knew just how diplomatic Alison could be—with children. For a moment Juanita protested, and then fell quiet as Pablo headed down towards the barn.

'Michael,' Alison commanded. The old sheep-dog stirred and came over beside them. In her schoolgirl Spanish, Alison explained; Juanita struggled with the language, but the message, and the soft, trusting eyes of the old dog, seemed to get through. An hour later, remembering, Alison found a pair of her old Raggedy-Ann dolls to add to the heap. Another hour brought mealtime, and pan-fried chicken legs, and by that time the two females were on the best of terms.

At one that afternoon the plumber's truck arrived. The movable feast was transferred from the kitchen to the veranda, and the pair of them set up shop on the swing.

Four big, bronzed men walked the side of the ditch, screwing the ends of the pipe together, sealing the joints, making a water pathway in their slow but steady manner, singing as they came closer to the house. And as they came Alison explained it all. What she herself didn't understand, she faked. Juanita chuckled and giggled and relaxed, and before the men were half-way down the hill the child was asleep with her head on Alison's lap.

'Gibson,' the foreman of the crew introduced himself, standing with one foot on the bottom step, his ten-gallon hat in hand. 'Suppose you want the pipe connected to the storage tank?'

'Yes,' Alison answered softly. 'The tank is in the attic. I think it's full. I don't think I want to switch over until everything is ready.'

'Everything's ready,' he reported. 'Got me two men on t'other end of the windmill. Jus' give me a minute here, while we shut off the old well, an' we'll drain the tank and change over. Take us about twenty minutes. Little girl's pooped, huh?'

'She had a hard night. Big party and all,' Alison said. 'I—don't suppose you need to talk to me about—money?' And if you do, I don't know what I'll do, she thought desperately. I could be honest and tell you to stop, that it's all a con game, but I want that clean water *so* badly!

'Nothin' to talk about,' he said. 'All paid for. Somebody in town. I don't rightly know who. Got in late this morning, and didn't check with the office.'

'Thank heaven,' Alison sighed, and then remembered her hospitality. 'I don't dare get up and leave the child, but I set a pitcher of lemonade and another of iced tea out on the kitchen-table. You'll all help yourselves?'

'Don't mind if we do, ma'am.' He tipped his hat and went back to his crew. The clangour of the piping didn't seem to bother Juanita, but it did affect the crows that nested in the plane trees. They rose on a storm of wings, complained raucously, and went down to the barn. Perhaps it wasn't the pipes. Perhaps it was the ranch truck coming sedately up the drive, with Steady Colson driving.

He stopped his car just in front of the steps and came around hurriedly to help Carmen out. The Guatemalan woman was all smiles as she clutched the baby tightly against her breast.

'So soon the car goes, the baby sleeps,' she said. 'The other one, too?'

'Out like a light.' Alison giggled. 'She likes watching men do hard labour.'

'Now maybe you can tell me,' Steady said as he came up the steps to join them. 'All of a sudden your—housekeeper?'

'Yes. Carmen,' Alison said.

'Yes. All of a sudden your Carmen seems to have lost control of her English. I've asked four times what the child's problem was, and she can't seem to explain it.'

'You don't speak Spanish?' Alison asked cautiously.

'You asked me that once before. I own exactly six words in Spanish,' he admitted. 'But that's not Spanish she's speaking!'

'Ah,' Alison said, easing Juanita's head off her lap so she could stand up. The little girl continued to sleep. 'I'll bet you're thirsty?'

'*Sí,*' Carmen said.

'Why do I get the idea that I'm being put off?' he asked.

'I can't imagine.' Alison laughed. 'Just a minute.' In quick and not entirely grammatical Quiché she warned Carmen not to make any startling revelations. The housekeeper, in the same language, gave her a quick résumé of the troubles. Alison nodded.

'Her mother says it's a recurrence of an old injury,' she translated for his benefit, mixing truth and fiction liberally. 'The muscles, you know. Occasionally she has a relapse, and requires therapy. There's nothing terribly important involved—just a little massage and things like that. Oh, and the language is a Mayan dialect. Carmen comes from Guatemala. Now, if the inquisition is concluded?'

'Well, I *am* sorry,' he said. 'I put the cart before the horse, I guess. A habit of mine. Another habit I have is that I'm intensely curious.'

'We've noticed. Now, about that cool drink?'

Juanita woke up at that moment. Colson walked over to the swing with a big, welcoming smile on his face. The girl immediately slid off on to the floor, ducked around him, and hid herself behind Carmen's skirts.

'I think I take the children to our quarters,' Carmen said. 'Maybe they don't have enough rest. We are up late two nights in a row, you understand. Tired makes them shy, no?'

Without waiting for an agreement, she shooed the two children in front of her into the house and down the corridor to their own quarters.

'*Now* I'll have that drink,' Colson said. Alison gave him a wary look. If there was anything about him she was sure of, it was that the more innocuous he appeared, the more dangerous he was. Trying not to appear too suspicious, she led the way into the house and back to the kitchen.

Mr Gibson was there, standing at the sink. 'All done, ma'am,' the plumber announced. 'The switch-over is complete. Your attic pressure-tank is filling from the new well now. I'd recommend you let it fill, then drain it again. To rinse out the tank, so to speak.'

'Why—I thank you,' Alison said. 'It'll be wonderful having drinkable water in the house. You know Mr Colson, I suppose?'

'Can't say as I do,' the plumber replied. Alison watched both their faces for some clue. There was none. As best she could tell, the two men were complete strangers. So it *had* to be the committee that had paid for all this? A wonderful gift, of course, she admitted to herself, but I'll just have to say something when next we meet!

'Where do you go when you disappear like that?' Colson asked. Startled, Alison refocused her eyes on him. Gibson grinned at both of them and made himself scarce.

'I—didn't even have a chance to thank him,' Alison complained.

'But you did have a chance to evade my question again.' Colson chuckled. 'You are without a doubt a world-class evader.'

'If I knew what you're talking about, and if I understood what you meant, I——' Alison gave him a stormy look. 'And you don't have any right to question me about my life!' she concluded with a snap.

'No, I don't suppose I do,' he sighed. 'It's not enough, is it, that we're neighbours? That we have a sincere interest in a pipeline. That you have two lovely children that I could fall in love with so easily——'

'They're not mine, they're Carmen's,' Alison interrupted sternly.

'But you love them as if they were yours,' he stated. 'Now, where was I? Oh, while I'm at it, my mother will tell you that I hate to be interrupted. I have enough trouble following a thought around, without other people sticking a spoke in my way.'

'Why, you——' Alison sputtered.

'Exactly.' His laugh, and that impossible grin, spilled all the anger out of her sails. She found herself grinning back.

'But then, you know my mother,' he continued. 'I would love to have been able to overhear *that* conversation between you two. My mother loves me, you know.'

'I've heard that's common among mothers,' Alison responded, trying her best to be solemn. 'A sort of disease that they can't help.'

It was hard to imagine a grown, hulking man looking like a hurt little boy, but he did. 'You sure know how to stab a guy in the back,' he complained.

'I don't, but I'm learning.'

'Yeah, well. That's another thing we have in common. My mother thinks you're the finest filly to come down the pike in a dog's age. How about that?'

Behave yourself, Alison told herself. This is not some ranch-hand, he's a barracuda. Give him one little clue, and we're all wasted! But it was hard to hold back. 'Well,' she said judiciously, 'I've been told by others that I'm a particularly nice woman to know.'

'Oh, lord,' he muttered. 'Isn't it enough that you're all that, without boasting? Can't you see that, if we're to make a go of it together, you have to recognise that I have a monstrous ego which needs to be pampered?'

Alison Springer had a round dozen things she wanted to say—gentle comments which might set him down as he deserved. Unfortunately, he leaned across the table and kissed her, and all her thoughts went out of the window.

Kissing him was fun. That she realised after the first impact. It was no longer him doing the kissing. Her hands went up around his neck and she leaned into the work. He tasted like lemonade and warmth and passion, and she had hardly ever tried that combination before. But there was only so much breath an inexperienced girl could do without. She came up out of the explosion with the strange feeling that her bare foot was cold.

'Oh, dear.' She wrestled herself away. For a strong man he seemed to be terribly weak—suddenly. There was a dazed look in his eyes, as if he had paid for a penny kiss and gotten ten-dollars' worth.

'Oh, dear, what?' he managed to get out. Alison waved towards the sink. The water was spurting from the tap with a life she hadn't seen in years. And the sink drain was still performing the stately pavane that had suited the household and the cesspool. As a result, the sink was overflowing, and cold, delicious drinking water was turning the linoleum kitchen into a swimming-pool.

'Oh, dear,' Alison repeated as she skidded over and turned the tap off. 'Mr Colson——'

'I know.' He held up both hands in a gesture of surrender. 'Even my mother would tell me it's time to leave.'

'Or grab a mop,' she suggested.

'That liberated, I am not.' He chuckled. 'See you tomorrow, redhead.'

'Nobody calls me that,' she shouted after his retreating back, but it was too late. She stood in the middle of her wet floor and considered.

'I'm going to have to get a score-card,' she murmured as she leaned on her wet mop.

'What you do there?' Carmen came in hurriedly and snatched the mop from her unresisting hands.

'Well, it's not red,' Alison said wonderingly. 'Russet, maybe. Not red!' Her hand went up to her face, and two fingers touched where his lips had been. She left them there for a moment, and then vigorously scrubbed, as if to rid herself of the dream.

CHAPTER FOUR

A WEEK was required for life to settle back to normal on the Springer ranch. Carmen became her usual chatterbox. Pablo returned to his livestock, and the children came to life. But Steady Colson didn't come at all, and Alison was not sure whether that was a blessing or a curse.

She worked hard on a new idea: the doctor had recommended swimming for Conchita. Down in the lowland area past the barn, a little stream tumbled down off the escarpment, huddled for a moment in a shallow sandy-bottom pool, and then plunged over a four-foot waterfall on its way to the Medina River. Using her own mare as a power source, and a set of chains, Alison hauled some of the area's large scattered stones into a loose sort of dam, and managed to increase the depth of the pool until it was suitable for swimming. It was not the ideal dam construction. Water squirrelled through countless little holes. But it made a pleasantly cool place. The cluster of old weeping willows, their roots steeped in what had once been a swamp, provided shade from the sun, and yet left room for the breezes to blow.

It was here, on a couple of old blankets, that Alison and the two children were picnicking when Steady Colson finally showed. He rode that magnificent palomino again, and Harriet Glebe was beside him on the roan.

'Hi, y'all,' he called from the saddle.

Alison grinned up at him. 'A little more practice and you'll sound like a Texan,' she said. 'Miss Glebe.' The

68

children, awed by the horses, moved closer to Alison.
There were no skirts for them to hide behind. Allie was
wearing a very impractical bikini. She hadn't expected
company, especially not male company, otherwise she
would never have taken the darn thing out of the drawer.
It had been her final foolish purchase some years earlier
when she came through Corpus Christi.

Not only was it skimpy, but it had the colossal nerve
to be light tan in colour, perfectly matching her skin.
As a result, from a distance of two or three yards it gave
the impression she was wearing nothing at all! Well, at
least my face is red enough for contrast, she thought as
she scrambled for a bath towel and did her best to cover
up.

'Now there's no need for that,' he chortled. Alison
gave him a disgusted look. It barely matched the one
Harriet Glebe was aiming at him. He seemed to be im-
pervious to both death-wishes as he swung down out of
the saddle and assisted his partner—accomplice, Alison
thought—to dismount.

'A lovely little place,' Harriet Glebe said. Her voice
was frosty enough to discourage even a simpleton from
taking the words at face value. 'And what delightful
children.'

It required a great deal of strength for Alison to re-
frain from saying, 'Yes, they've both had their dis-
temper shots! You could even touch one of them if you
felt like it!' Instead, she mustered up a thin-lipped
agreement.

'Easy, easy there,' Steady said. Alison looked around,
expecting that he was talking to his horse. Instead he
was grinning straight at her! Counting to ten was just
not going to do. Gritting her teeth and dropping her

towel, she did a racing dive into the pool, steamed across and back at full speed, and then rejoined them.

'A little penance there?' He was standing at the edge of the water holding her towel. She slipped it around her shoulders. He was close enough to the truth to warrant a little smile.

'Possibly, Mr Colson,' she said. 'What brings you to the Springer spread today?'

'Oh, just neighbourliness,' he replied. 'Harriet has been so busy in court these past few days, she hasn't had a chance to ride out and relax.'

'Crime's rampant?' Alison asked as she settled the two little girls down again at their lunch.

'Smuggling,' Harriet reported. Steady had found a place to sit, in between the two girls, and they had accepted him despite the language barrier. The palomino stood in place; the roan was restless, and Miss Glebe had tied him to one of the tree branches. She refused to sit down, and stood impatiently, tapping one end of her riding crop into the palm of her other hand. 'Smuggling,' she repeated. 'There seems to be a great deal of it going around. I was looking at some very interesting records at the county sheriff's office.'

'Were you really? I've got potato salad and sweetcorn left,' Alison offered, hoping to change the subject. 'Unfortunately the hot dogs are all gone. These two little mites seem to be empty down to both legs!' She explained to the children with exaggerated gestures and a few words in Quiché, and sent them into spasms of laughter.

'You have a good command of their language,' Steady commented.

'Contrary-wise,' Alison answered. 'It's because I have an atrocious accent and a limited vocabulary that they're laughing so hard! If you want to hear pure Quiché, you must listen to Pablo——'

'Well?' Harriet interrupted. She was about to continue with her private little vendetta when she caught a glimpse of the baby's leg. 'Why—that poor child is a cripple,' she said as she drew back from both children.

'That's not a word we use,' Alison said fiercely. 'Children don't need to be reminded of what they are. Conchita is a perfectly normal little child who happens to have had an accident!'

Steady Colson bent over the baby. Conchita was dressed in a nappy and rubber pants, just enough to cover her bottom, and the scar on her leg looked tremendous. 'An old wound,' he diagnosed. 'Gunshot?'

'No, of course not.' Alison hurried to get her denials in. 'Just an accident. A terrible one, but just an accident.' She picked the baby up, turned her back on the others, and walked down to the water. Juanita, eyes as big as saucers, followed along.

Allie carried the child out just far enough so that when she was placed face-down in the water her hands touched the bottom and allowed her head to be up, while her feet trailed off into the deeper area. The baby showed no fear, but, just in case, her sister sat down in front of her, teasing, while Alison gently manipulated the tiny legs. After a moment Conchita caught the rhythm and began to kick for herself, squealing in delight as she did so.

The game was carefully timed. Three minutes of kicking, two to rest, and then back to the kicking-cycle. Gradually the rate slowed as the baby tired. Before she could overdo it, Alison snatched her up out of the water, and congratulated her with a big hug. Conchita enjoyed the game, it was plain to see, but the water was cool and she was ready to come out. Alison carried her back to the blankets, wrapped her up in a big towel, and sat down to gently massage both the leg and the child's back. Meanwhile the older sister, already well-trained for swimming, paddled around within call, enjoying herself.

'You look as if you had achieved your life's ambition,' Steady said.

'One of them,' Alison agreed. 'When you do something good for a child, you make a huge investment in the future. Would you watch Juanita for me? Sometimes she gets too brave for her boots.'

There was a little game that went with the massage. A 'peek-a-boo' routine in which the child's head was covered with the towel while Alison loudly searched for her. And when finally the cover was pulled from her head, Conchita giggled madly and demanded more. Finally Alison spun her out of the towel and gently applied soothing oil to the leg and to the child's back.

'You're not the child's mother,' Harriet remarked. 'Why don't you let *her* do that stuff.'

'Because I was trained to do *that stuff*,' Alison replied gently. 'I'm a registered nurse. It's only a little thing I'm doing. You could learn—oh, I forgot. You're already a lawyer. I suppose that's a useful occupation, too?'

'I resent the comparison!' Harriet snapped. 'Comparing a lawyer to a—nurse? Good lord!'

'Yes, I suppose that's true, too,' Alison chuckled. 'Only I hope that if you ever need a nurse you aren't surrounded by lawyers!' She smiled to herself, what she thought was a private smile, but which really gave her a Mona Lisa look. The baby was beginning to complain. 'Juanita? *Vámonos, querida!*'

The older sister came out of the water reluctantly. Colson offered a hand to steady her, and to Alison's surprise the girl took it and held on for dear life.

When they got back to the blankets Steady picked up another towel, wrapped Juanita in it, and dried her. The child dressed herself with great solemnity.

'You know something, Alison Springer?' he said as he watched.

'No, what?' She was still too busy with the baby to look up. If she had, she would have seen an admiring look on his face.

'I'll tell you what,' he said. 'You've got a heart as big as Texas.'

That stopped Alison in her tracks. One hand on the baby's stomach kept the child from rolling away while she looked at him over her shoulder, considering. 'Why, that's one of the nicest things anyone has ever said to me,' she replied. Her heart was in her eyes. She blinked her long, curly lashes down to hide the message, but from the way his face lit up she knew she had been too late! Immediately she felt the pain. The lion does *not* lie down with the lamb, she told herself, and schooled her face.

'Come on, Stedman,' Harriet Glebe interrupted. 'I wanted to get a good ride, not watch an episode of *Happy Families*!'

'Yes, well,' he sighed as he followed the tall, thin blonde over to where the horses were standing. 'Duty calls, and all that. Alison?'

'What?'

'My mother wants you to come and call—and bring the kids, of course.'

'I'm—not sure that I can,' Alison replied. Her hands were still busy with the baby, and for a moment she didn't quite know what to say. 'We're so busy. And there's so much to do——' And I don't want to get too embroiled with you, Mr Stedman Colson, nor with that fiancée of yours. Oil and water don't mix. And neither do smugglers and prosecutors!

'You *want* to come,' he insisted as he swung easily up into the saddle.

'*Want's* a hard taskmaster,' she answered softly. He gave her a puzzled look, and offered to take Juanita up before him in the saddle. The older girl was eager for the ride. Harriet Glebe intended no such courtesy for the baby, so Alison wrapped the child up again in a towel and carried her along between the two animals. They were just passing the corral outside the barn when Killer, the rodeo horse, started on one of his patented demonstrations.

'Hey, look at that!' Colson said in amazement. Carmen, who had been feeding the chickens, came over to join them.

'One mad horse,' the housekeeper said. 'Nobody ride that one, no? Not even Pablo, and he the best rider in Texas. That horse, he got a devil in him.'

Alison, with her eyes locked on Steady Colson, took a deep breath. It was almost as if she could read the man's mind through his face! Nobody can ride that horse? I can ride that horse, the man was thinking.

'Oh, no!' she gasped. 'You—don't understand. Killer is a——'

'My maw used to sing me an old song,' he said as he passed Juanita down to her mother and swung himself out of the saddle. 'How's it go, now? "There's never a horse that couldn't be rode"? I forget the rest of it.'

'But—but riding in California isn't like riding in Texas,' Alison told him. 'This horse is——'

'Never a horse that couldn't be rode,' he repeated. That challenging grin was back on his face. He looked through the bars of the corral like a boy admiring a triple ice-cream sundae.

'Stedman Colson,' Harriet thundered. 'I don't intend to stay here and watch you make a fool of yourself!'

'No, and I wouldn't want you to,' Colson replied. 'Why don't you ride on ahead and tell my mother we'll join her for dinner?'

It must have been the unexpected dinner invitation that did it. Harriet Glebe nibbled on her lip for a moment, then wheeled her mount, rowelled him with her spurs, and galloped off.

Pablo had come out of the barn to join the discussion. 'Mean,' he commented. 'No need to spur a horse like that. What's up?'

'Mr Colson here thinks that Killer needs a little workout, and that he's the man to do it,' Alison said cautiously. 'Maybe you could talk him out of it? He was mentioning something about an old song.'

'There's never a horse that couldn't be rode,' Colson repeated with absolute assurance. 'I didn't learn my horsemanship on a movie lot.'

'But——'

'Now, Miss Alison, if the man's determined, the likes of us shouldn't be trying to discourage him.' Pablo shook his head solemnly. His wife pinched his elbow. 'Folks pay a lot of money to see people ride Killer.'

'All right,' Alison sighed. 'But you'd better be very careful—Steady!'

'That's my middle name—Careful.' He chuckled. 'Pablo, will you give me a hand getting him saddled?'

'Don't mind if I do!' The two men grinned at each other.

'What you do?' the obviously worried Carmen muttered at her husband.

'Just a ride,' Pablo said. 'Nothin' for you women to worry about.'

'Nothing at all,' Alison said in a worried undertone.

'Dos hombres locos,' Carmen said. 'He gonna bust his head!' She threw up her hands in disgust as the two madmen vaulted over the top rail into the corral, and cornered the horse.

Saddling Killer was not as difficult as Alison had expected. One never knew, with an animal like this, what to expect. In this case the big stallion submitted with easy grace. Alison had a quick flash of intuition. The animal intended to save his strength for the main test! He was still standing peacefully when Steady Colson swung up into the saddle and Pablo made a mad dash for the fence.

The horse even took a couple of gentle prancing steps, as if his eight-year reputation for mayhem was all a dirty lie. 'About that song,' Allie prodded. Pablo looked down at her and grinned.

'"Ain't never a horse that couldn't be rode, ain't never a cowpoke who couldn't be throwed,"' he quoted.

'Oh, my lord,' Alison groaned. Killer took the words to be the signal to begin.

From a standing start, with both legs rigid on the ground, Killer went straight up into the air, spun around, came down with a tremendous crash, and began bucking back and forth across the corral. Occasionally, to vary the performance, he would rear, threaten to go over backwards, and then come down hard and try to buck the rider off over his head.

Steady Colson was a strong rider, but he had seen too many Western movies. His stetson came off, he gave a wild yip of encouragement, and he waved the hat a time or two by the horse's head. Killer stopped to consider the fool on his back. That was the moment that Steady Colson kicked him with both heels. The horse snorted, took a deep breath, went up into the air and turned eastward before landing.

Steady Colson, yelling his heart out, went up with the horse, lost both his stirrups, and when Killer turned eastward Steady continued on west. There came a reasonably large crash as the man bounced off the outer wall of the barn and collapsed in a pile of hay strewn in the corner. Killer, his day's work done, became a very casual horse, nibbling a straw or two before seeking the watering trough.

Pablo was over the fence almost as soon as Steady landed. Alison took a moment longer. It was difficult to climb a shaven wooden corral bar with speed when one was wearing a bikini. There was a tendency to acquire splinters in some unfortunate places. But she *did* hurry.

'I shouldn't have let him!' she said bitterly as she came up to Pablo's side.

'He done well for a California man,' Pablo retorted. 'You couldn't have stopped him. That man's got more "stubborn" than a brace of mules.' At their feet, Steady Colson opened both eyes and managed a very weak smile.

'I do believe I misjudged the animal,' he said, putting both hands to his forehead in a shaky fashion. 'I—seem to have a little trouble.'

'Did you break a leg or something?' Pablo asked in a very matter-of-fact tone.

'Oh, my,' Alison gasped. She dropped to her bare knees on the rough ground and began to run both hands up and down his legs, his arms, his torso in a very professional manner.

'*Madre de Dios,*' Carmen groaned. Little Juanita, in her mother's arms, chattered away in Quiché.

'What did she say?' Colson asked, wincing as he tried to move himself into a more comfortable position.

'She wanted to know,' Alison said bleakly, 'if you could do that again. She thought it was very funny! Move your right leg.'

'I don't see the humour of it at all,' he complained dolefully.

'Shut up,' she commanded. The drill went on; each arm, each finger, each leg, each toe. Her hands shook a little as she unbuttoned his shirt, exposed his broad chest, and probed at his ribs. 'Does that hurt?'

He had his lips locked, and there was devilry in his eyes.

'Well?'

'You told me to shut up,' he muttered. 'If I had known you were a nurse, I wouldn't have come within a hundred miles of you. Bossiest women in the world, nurses.'

'Oh, shut up!' Her hands ranged over his ribcage again, applying a little more pressure. He continued to smile. Compelled by some feeling she could not explain, Alison leaned over and kissed him just above his heart.

'That's nice,' he commented. 'Mommy's kissing it better?'

'Don't be silly!' she snapped. 'That's standard medical technology. Now let me see your head.'

'Naughty, naughty,' he said, chuckling. 'You could lose your licence for telling lies to patients.'

'Oh, shut up,' she sighed, and ran her fingers through his thick hair. The bump was low on the back of his head. Not terribly big, but in a bad place. It was the sort of condition where a wise nurse waits for a doctor, she told herself. But then she remembered her year in the Peace Corps, where the nearest doctor might be five hundred miles away, and a sensible nurse did everything except brain surgery!

'Close your eyes.' Her fingers came down over his eyelids and helped force them shut. She counted. Long enough for the pupils of his eyes to cycle. 'Now, open them both.'

He did. She watched closely. The pupil of his right eye adjusted to the light; that of the left reacted much more slowly. Confirmation of a guess—the process that a solemn medical man would call apt diagnosis.

'You've got a bump on your head,' she said, shifting her weight off her uncomfortable knees to her heels.

Again that watery smile. 'Thank you, doctor. I *had* noticed that myself.'

'You've already been a jackass once today,' she returned, 'so there's no need to do it again. I think you have a concussion.'

'We'd better get him up to the house,' Pablo volunteered. 'We have that old wheelchair of your grandmother's.'

'He a big man,' Carmen said. 'Well, I take the children to the house.'

'And the horse,' Alison added. 'That beautiful horse.'

The Chicano couple stared at her as if she had lost all her marbles. '*His* horse,' she explained. 'That beautiful palomino. You go along, too, Pablo, and bring the chair down. I'll stay with Mr Colson to keep him company.'

'OK, but first I'll put Killer back in his stall.'

Dr Pedillo finished his examination with aplomb, despite the fact that he was inwardly a bowl of jelly. A rotund little man who had given up smoking only after a long desperate battle with his wife, he had been astounded when the Colson ranch had sent a helicopter into the city to pick him up.

'Probably nothing more than a slight concussion,' he announced as he put his stethoscope away. 'Stay in bed for twenty-four hours. Eat lightly. If he starts to throw up, call me immediately.'

'We should take him in to the hospital,' Harriet Glebe declared.

'Nonsense,' Abigail Colson said. 'He's perfectly comfortable here. Plenty of room, a nurse at hand, close enough to home. What more could he ask——?'

'Well, I think that's the problem,' the patient interrupted. 'I haven't been asked.'

Three pairs of eyes turned towards Alison. No, her conscience dictated. Keep him as far away from here as possible! But her mouth was on a swivel, with a mind of its own. 'Of course he can stay,' she heard herself say. And then she compounded the problem. 'And you, too, Mrs Colson—Abigail. If you wish.'

'No, no,' the old lady said. 'I couldn't think of it. I have a dozen things to do at home. Not quite settled in, you know. Besides, you will take good care of him.'

'In that case, I think I'll stay,' Harriet Glebe announced.

'I suppose he *could* go in to Baptist Hospital,' Dr Pedillo said, trying to throw a little oil on troubled waters. The oil promptly caught fire. The patient groaned.

'There,' his mother declared. 'He can't possibly be moved. Absolutely not. I forbid it. And I don't think it's a good idea for you to stay, Harriet. You might disturb him.'

'Either he goes to hospital, or I stay with him,' Miss Glebe said belligerently.

Alison looked from one woman to the other, her mind completely in a whirl. Mrs Colson had something on her mind besides her only son's health. But what? Why would she be going to all this trouble to see that Steady remained at the Springer ranch, preferably with only Alison Springer in attendance? On the other hand, Harriet Glebe's position was quite clear. For some mad reason she seemed to think that Alison Springer was competition for *her* man, and she intended to stay close to the bedside just to make sure! Allie, who looked in her mirror about as much as any woman, knew how ridiculous the idea was. What there was of Springer beauty had skipped her entirely. Too short, compared to her tall, thin grandmother; too—curvy, when compared to her long-lost mother; too opinionated when compared to almost any female in Texas! Oh, well, she finally decided, I might just as well take the bitter with the bitter. And having thus ruined a perfectly good cliché, she shared a sunny smile with all of them. 'Why not? We have plenty of room. Anybody who wants to stay over is welcome.'

'I knew you were a common-sense lass when I first met you!' Mrs Colson gathered up her bag, kissed her son, and patted Alison's cheek as she went by on her way to the door. The doctor followed along, tugging at a black bag that was almost too heavy for him to carry.

'Remember, if he starts to throw up, call me.'

'I will,' Alison agreed. The helicopter pilot was standing on the porch. In a moment the engine roared, leaving a cloud of dust behind.

'I've got to do something about that dust,' Alison said as she turned her attention to her guest. 'Now then, Miss

Glebe. Suppose we put you in the corner room, where you'll be away from the children and their noises?'

'Suppose we put me in the room right next door?' Harriet said grimly. Battle is joined, Alison told herself. So that's what jealousy does to a woman? Luckily, I don't have any such feelings. So why am I so upset about Harriet being in the room next door? She opened her mouth to argue the case, but a quick look at the patient cut off the debate. The darn coward had gone to sleep. Well, it *looked* as if he were sleeping, but then—who knew?

'Why, what a good idea that is,' she told Harriet. 'Come along. I'll get sheets and things together. You did bring some things with you?'

'No, I didn't,' Harriet replied. 'But I'm sure you can loan me something.'

'I—doubt that.' Alison looked her up and down. 'You look to be five foot eleven, and I'm only five four.'

'Five foot ten and a half,' Harriet gloated. 'Just a half-inch shorter than Stedman! Isn't that wonderful?'

'I suppose so,' Alison murmured. One of the patient's eyes was half-open. The dirty rat, she thought. Hiding out to avoid the battle! A deep-dyed double-dipped yellow-belly! Well, Mr Colson, there isn't going to *be* any battle, she fumed under her breath! 'Yes, you must be lucky, having so much in common with—Stedman. But perhaps you could call the Colson ranch and have them send some of your clothes up? It shouldn't take but a half-hour.'

'You mean you have a telephone in this—place?'

'Why, yes, indeed.' Alison touched her cheek to make sure the smile hadn't fallen off. 'And running water, and an indoor bath. Only one, by the way, for the whole crowd of us. I hope you won't mind?'

'I'll try to make do,' Harriet said as she sat down on one of the straight-backed chairs. Gran Springer had furnished the bedroom from her own ideas of utility. Bedrooms were made to hold beds, and that was the most comfortable thing in the room. Chairs in bedrooms were only needed when one wanted to take off one's shoes—or a place to throw clothing as one took it off. So chairs could be straight, hard, and uncomfortable. The three chairs in the room met the prescription.

'But it's four o'clock, you know,' the tall blonde continued. 'I'm accustomed to a tea-break along about this time. Perhaps you could arrange it while I watch Stedman.'

'Why, of course,' Alison murmured. 'How gross of me not to think of that without being reminded!' She rushed out of the room, anxious to be out of sight when the giggles broke out. She made it to the kitchen, and burst in on an astonished Carmen.

'Tea,' Alison managed to squeeze out through tears of laughter. 'La-di-dah. We have tea each day at four! Whoops, my dear!'

'Tea?' Carmen asked doubtfully. 'I don't know we got any tea. Everybody drinks coffee, no? Maybe she means coffee?'

'No, she means tea. That old canister way in the back—no, on the bottom shelf. Gran used to keep it for visitors.'

'Must be five—six years old,' Carmen muttered.

'Yes, but we're using new water,' Alison replied, doing her best to keep a straight face.

'Ah? Every day I learn something. Cookies?'

'I suppose,' Alison sighed. The fun had suddenly gone out of things. Harriet was jealous for no reason. Steady Colson was a dangerous male. Alison Springer was being a fool to let her mind wander, even for a minute, in his direction. For just a little time, she told herself, she had slipped out from under that tremendous load of duty that weighed her shoulders down. Just for a little time—and now it was back, pressing her youth into a tiny bundle, stretching a future in front of her that promised only more of the same.

'Tea's ready,' Carmen announced. 'You don't look good, missy.'

'I'm—just tired,' Alison said. 'I'll take it in. Do we have enough for supper?'

'Lamb stew. What you like. I put three more potatoes in, some carrots, like that?'

'Sounds great.' Alison picked up the tray, wondering why it had become so heavy. 'Did Conchita react all right?'

'Straight to bed for nap,' Carmen said. 'Best thing to happen to this child. Massage every day?'

'Every day. And swimming as long as the water's not too cool. She won't fight it? I have trouble understanding what she says.'

'Everybody have trouble with two-years-old,' Carmen said, comforting her. 'That child, she gonna grow up an' be illiterate in three languages.'

'Well, just as long as she understands that we all love her,' Alison sighed, 'no matter what language we have to use. Here I go. Wish me luck.'

The tray seemed to get heavier at every step. And even worse when she came in the bedroom door. Steady was awake, sitting slightly propped up with two pillows behind him.

'Well, it certainly took long enough,' Harriet complained. The woman had evidently spent some time primping. Although still dressed in her jodhpurs and blouse, she was as neat and as sleek as a Persian cat. *While I look like something dragged through the hedge backwards,* Alison thought.

'It takes a little longer,' Allie told them both. Once again she had decided to brazen it out. 'We have a special tea, a blend of Indian and Chinese, you know. Gran had it imported directly from Szechwan province.' *And don't for heaven's sake tell them how long ago!* 'Would you clear that side-table, Harriet?'

The blonde moved reluctantly, setting the little table beside the bed where Steady could have direct access to it. She moved her own chair, too, and immediately assumed the role of hostess.

'Cream, Stedman?'

'That's—not cream,' Alison apologised. 'We don't keep cream. That's milk. I hope——'

'There's nothing I like better than plain milk in my tea,' Steady contributed. Harriet gave him a smile, as if she were being complimented.

'And no lemon?'

'And no lemon,' Alison muttered. 'Wasn't that what we fought the Revolution about? So we wouldn't have to drink lemon in our tea?'

'Very funny,' Miss Glebe said. 'Please, sit down. Nothing irritates me more than people who hover over one.'

Put that away in your memory, Alison told herself. Zap. Nothing irritates Miss Glebe more than—I want to make a list. Irritating her is going to be my favourite sport! But she sat, anyway.

As expected, the tea tasted terrible. Even Steady grimaced at his first sip. Harriet groped for an acceptable phrase. 'My, that certainly is *something*,' she said.

'Very much so.' And isn't that a puzzle, Allie thought. Harriet sounds as if she means it! What have I done right?

'Excellent,' Steady added. 'Best tea I've tasted this year!'

'And now that I'm here,' Harriet said, 'there's something I want to talk to you about, Springer. Wait a second. I have the paper in my purse, and I left it on the veranda.'

'Springer?' Alison wondered aloud.

'Listen, while she's out of sight,' Steady whispered. 'I never drink tea. When she comes to my place, my mother slips me a cup of coffee on the sly. But as best I can remember the taste of tea, this is probably the worst blend I've ever been exposed to!'

'Probably,' Alison murmured, 'but you'll have to get used to it. Think of it as medicine. You know the medicine is no good for you if it tastes good. Springer, indeed! I haven't been called that since I graduated from nursing school. I take it you're feeling better?'

'It must have been the nap.'

Alison moved over to the bed and took his pulse. 'Nap, baloney,' she said. 'You can't fool a real nurse with a fake nap.'

'You know, you really have me scared,' he said. 'I never thought I would be dealing with a real nurse. Not ever in the world. How come you're out singing and dancing for a living, when you're a registered nurse?'

'Because, if it has escaped your notice,' she said primly, 'singing and dancing pay off a heck of a lot more by the hour than nursing does. You see the newspapers full of advertisements for nurses these days. If they took the advertising money and added it to a nurse's salary they'd be knee-deep in nurses! Besides, nursing is hard work. Imagine having to put in eight hours a day at the beck and call of three dozen people like you!'

'Hey, that's a low blow,' he protested. 'Is that any way to treat a patient? Tell me about the nursing.'

'There's nothing much to tell,' Alison said slowly. 'When I graduated from high school Gran talked me into enrolling in a two-year nursing programme at a junior college. I got my Associate's degree, and went immediately into the Peace Corps. When my assignment was up I came back here, but Gran needed me, so instead of finding a nursing assignment I stayed home with her.'

'And then she died, but you still kept on with the ranch?'

'More or less,' Alison said. 'There was always the challenge. This used to be a fine income-producing spread. And Pablo and Carmen and the children—I couldn't just abandon them, could I?'

'No, of course not.' He moved a little; she hurried to rearrange the pillows behind his back. 'As I said,' he chuckled, 'a heart as big as Texas! You wouldn't care to kiss me, I suppose?'

'What? With your girlfriend out in the other room? I *never* kiss patients—well, at least only the very little ones!' Zap. Take that, Stedman Colson. You didn't think the simple country girl would recognise that you're already taken? Huh! It might have been nice, though. Just one kiss.

'Ah. I have it here.' Harriet Glebe came back into the room, excitement turning her cheeks red. She was waving a computer print-out in her hands. 'It's starting to rain again. I wanted to show you this.' It was hard to tell whether she enjoyed the rain more than the paper. A real gloomy-gus, Allie concluded.

Harriet spread the paper out on the bed, showing Steady instead of Alison.

'Show me what?' Alison asked.

'This record sheet,' Harriet said, smacking her lips. 'It's a list of all actual and potential smuggling cases in Bexar County during the past three months. Look how many times the name Alison Springer shows up on it!'

CHAPTER FIVE

'I'M sorry I had to cut out on you like that last night,' Alison said as she joined Steady Colson on the broad veranda. 'Did you have a good breakfast?'

'Couldn't be better. Your Carmen took care of us like kings—well, king and queen. I take it you had your song-and-dance act last night?'

'Yes. A chiropractors' convention. They hired five barges in all, and kept at it until the wee hours. The tips were good, you know, but, lord, they were a handy people!'

'Oh, no—not that.' Steady leaned back among his cushions and grinned at her. 'Not puns at this hour of the day. Chiropractors—handy people.'

'I can't help it if I think that way,' she returned, glaring at him. 'Between dodging the pinchers and keeping out of the wet, it was just too much for my weak constitution. Where's your girlfriend?'

'If you mean Harriet Glebe, she had to go into town. She's a working girl, too, you know. And there are big things buzzing.'

Alison held up both hands. 'Please don't tell me about it,' she sighed. 'That girl is as convinced as the deputy sheriff that I'm smuggling something. So don't break down and let me in on any secrets!'

'Come over here.' He gestured to the footstool beside him. Alison moved slowly in that direction. Cautiously would have been a better word. There was some attraction about this man. No, he wasn't handsome, not

89

in the least. He was just—virile. And yet she dared not let down her guard. His friends were all on the wrong side of the law!

She had selected a lightweight cotton dress from her tiny wardrobe this morning. And that by itself was unusual. Ordinarily she worked her way around the spread in blue jeans and blouse. But this morning, awakened late by happy children's noises, she had opted for the multi-coloured sun-dress. Not that he's noticed, she told herself as she swept her skirts under her and sat down on the stool. 'You were going to tell me something?'

'I was going to tell you several somethings,' he said. 'First of all, though, no matter how many times the sheriff raids this place, I won't believe you're a smuggler. If you are, you must be the most inept smuggler in these United States. I've never seen a sorrier spread or a poorer bunch of people than y'all. Any reasonably successful smuggler would have the odour of money around him— or her, as the case may be.'

'Gee,' she said, wide-eyed, all innocence. 'Isn't that what they call damning with faint praise? Even the worst smugglers make a little money; I don't have *any* money; ergo, I can't be a smuggler?'

'I couldn't have said it better myself. You wouldn't care to kiss me this morning?'

'Not at this hour of the day,' she muttered. 'You seem to have sex on your mind all the time! I'd rather pun than kiss!'

'No,' he groaned. 'Suddenly my head hurts. It can only be cured by some more of that fresh homebaked bread.'

'Well, that's one thing I *can* provide.' Alison got up gracefully and whirled her way into the kitchen. Carmen and Pablo were huddled around the table.

'It's all right,' she cautioned in a low voice. 'The committee debated the problem until four this morning.' And had nothing at all to say about water-pipes and ditch-digging for the Springer spread, she reminded herself.

'An' what they say?' Carmen asked.

'We all agree. We have to hang in there. Nothing moves for the next two or three weeks. Everything is played open and above-board. There's only one real problem, Pablo. If he sees those sheep, he's going to smell a rat!'

'Crazy, this English,' Carmen grumbled. 'Sheep, rats——'

'Not a problem,' Pablo interrupted. 'Come on, Carmen. Keep up the head, no? I can keep the sheep away from the homestead, Miss Allie. I'm afraid you're right. Our mangy flock is about as believable as Santa Claus. He won't learn anything from the kids, but the sheep could give us away!'

'Yes, that's true,' Alison mused. 'In fact, he likes them very much. The kids, not the sheep. Maybe we could set Juanita on him? While he's here, of course. I wouldn't want to chase him away, but, on the other hand, I wouldn't want him to make a permanent base on our veranda. OK, troops? Everything normal! Big smiles, heads up! Only one person we need to watch out for, and——'

'And that his mama,' Carmen interrupted.

'No. I was thinking more of that Harriet Glebe.'

'Listen, girl, you don't see the nose on the face,' the Guatemalan woman continued. 'His mama, she out to get you married up, Alison Springer. Anybody with one eye can see that! *Cuidado, linda!*'

'Ain't nothin' to be afraid of,' Pablo said. 'Mighty nice man, that one. Plenty of savvy, plenty of money— what more could a girl ask for?'

'Oh, please, you're both blowing smoke,' Alison protested weakly. 'He's engaged to that Harriet Glebe! She told me so, and he won't deny it. And his mother told me she would *never* want him to marry a girl like me!' But wouldn't *that* be a nice ending to a terrible story? she told herself. Steady and I and three—maybe four children? No more song-and-dance acts, no more scraping from day to day. Lots of loving cheerfulness, lots of—but nice girls don't think about things like that, even though it's all over the television networks. The only three-letter word that still holds centre stage. S. E. X. See there? I may not *do* it, but at least I can spell it!

'Ha!' Carmen interjected. 'Why you day-dream like that? What you come in the kitchen for, anyway?'

'Oh, lord!' Alison stepped back into reality. 'Bread. He wanted some more homemade bread!' Well, at least that was his *second* choice!

'We got plenty bread,' Carmen said as she walked over to the oven to check. 'You come home late, you whip up batter for six loaves bread? At that hour of the night you make bread? I tell you a dozen times tortillas easier to make!'

'Of course.' Alison had her smile back in place again. 'It's my weekly trip to the psychoanalyst. I tell the batter all my problems, and then I beat the living daylights out of it, work out all my frustrations, and can go to bed and sleep. Can you slice that bread a little thicker? He's one very big man!'

All of which brought Alison Springer back out on the porch with a plate full of buttered bread, a mug for herself, and a pot of black coffee. She pushed a table over beside his chair, using her ample hip to accomplish it.

'Mmm,' he said. 'Smell that bread! I could kill for a baker who does that well. I'd even go further than that! I'd marry for a woman like that!'

'Well, Carmen's already married,' she told him. 'What the devil was that?' The noise had come up suddenly. Something soared just over the roof of the house and went clattering away into the distance, leaving a thin, slow-settling spray behind it.

'Helicopter, I believe.'

'I *know* it was a helicopter, dummy! What I want to know is what's it doing around *here*?' She leaned out beyond the banister of the veranda and grabbed at a handful of whatever it was that was falling. 'Look at that! Some sort of——'

'Seed,' he interrupted. 'They're spraying the area with some sort of seed. Just the right time for it: a slow, steady drizzle all night, and overcast this morning.'

She looked at him suspiciously. 'And, of course, you had nothing to do with it?'

'Who, me?' The trouble with being a big virile man was that, even when you were innocent, you tended to look guilty! Nobody could look more guilty than Steady Colson at that particular moment.

'Yes. Who, you? What kind of seed is it?'

'Fescue,' he said, without thinking—and then sputtered as his brain came into gear. 'Well, maybe it's fescue. I don't really know. Lawyers don't know a great deal about grass seed.'

'No, I don't suppose they do.' She shook her head at the nerve of the man. 'Eat your bread while it's still hot. I made it!' The boast was unintentional. It slipped out, surprising her more than it surprised him. Now, stop that, she commanded herself. Don't make things worse than they are. And then, as a *non sequitur*, 'How's your head this morning?'

'Before I gave up drinking, I'd awakened with a lot more pain than this,' he said. 'I don't feel as grouchy as the average bear, if that's what you want to know.'

'Good! Then I expect you could go home today.' At least, that's *one* way to cut down the tension, she told herself. I'll get him gone, as Gran used to say. But even then, we'd have to lay low. It isn't possible, is it, that in just twenty-four hours I've come to appreciate having him around the house? I *will* miss him.

Without really thinking, she bent over him and gently kissed the tip of his nose, just past the place where the bump was.

'Funny, how you can look closely at someone and not see,' she said, the tip of her finger replacing her lips. 'What happened?'

'Football,' he replied. His hand came up to trap her finger. 'Long ago and far away, so to speak. You have strong fingers.' He carried the finger down to his lips and kissed it.

She was too flustered to reply immediately. I need a head of angry steam, she thought, working on it. 'A nurse has to be strong,' she told him! 'I wish——' Good lord, I don't know what I wish, and if I did know, I'd be a fool to tell him!

'I wish——?'

'Nothing,' she replied. 'Eat the bread. When are you and Miss Glebe going to get married?'

He settled back in his chair and laughed. 'So that's what the problem is?'

'There isn't any problem!' she snapped pettishly. 'Just idle curiosity. You don't *have* to tell me.'

He paused long enough to sample the bread. 'Mmm, good! You say *you* made this?'

'I made it,' she said.

'Hey, that's great,' he returned. 'My offer is still good. I'm not sure about when Harriet and I might get married. The subject has never come up.'

Which is about as close as he'll ever come to plain truth, Alison thought. 'What offer is that?'

'I said I'd marry the woman who could make bread like this!'

'Oh, come off it!' she snapped. 'That's not funny at all. What time would you like to go home? Or shall I call your mother and ask?'

'No, don't do that,' he called after her as she swished into the house, but the warning came too late.

The telephone rang four or five times before somebody picked it up. There was a background of conversation, as if the room down at the Colson spread was crowded. And then Abigail answered.

'This is Alison,' she said. 'You remember? Alison Springer?'

'Of course I remember, my dear. How could I forget? Has something happened to Steady?'

'Well, no, not exactly. It's just that he's so healthy that I thought—well, I wondered if he wouldn't feel better at home, and so I——'

'Heavenly days!' Abigail said, surprised. 'I had thought sure he would want to stay for a few days, so I told Harriet she could certainly bring her friends out here, and now the house is full.'

'Friends,' Alison asked weakly.

'More like business acquaintances,' Abigail said. 'You know, it's convention time in the city, and getting a place to stay is difficult. So when the Federal and the State Government planned this massive round-up of smugglers, they were short of space to house the agents. We have eight of them here now, and two more coming. If Steady comes back today he'll have to sleep in the barn!'

'Ten agents!' Alison's tongue kept sticking to the roof of her mouth. Fear; raw, unadulterated fear. Ten agents, only four miles from her door. Massive round-up. Oh, hell!

'Alison? Alison, are you still there?'

'Yes, I'm here, Mrs—Abigail. I didn't know. Steady didn't tell me anything, and——'

'Oh, dear,' Abigail said. 'Have I—what is it they say in the movies? Have I blown their cover?'

'No. I don't think so. I wouldn't say anything. I—suppose Steady can stay here. But—do you have any idea how long?'

'Not long, dear. Everything is planned. About four days, maybe five. Would that be inconvenient?'

'No, not at all,' Alison lied. 'Not at all!'

'Let him play with those children,' Abigail offered as a parting shot. 'He's a fool about kids, my son is. I *do* so wish he'd get married.' The sigh that floated down the wires was sobering.

'Yes, I suppose he will when he's ready,' Alison replied. 'Or when Harriet tells him he's ready.'

'Ha!' Mrs Colson said, not at all pleasantly, and slammed down the telephone.

So maybe I'm dense, Alison thought as she walked slowly back out on to the veranda. Mrs Colson isn't too happy about Steady marrying Harriet. That doesn't mean that *I'm* the new candidate. But if he does get me to the altar, I'll go kicking and screaming all the way! It isn't enough that he could put me in jail for ten thousand years, he's also the most aggravating man in the world. He thinks all he has to do is say the word and I'll fall right into his arms! Or at his feet. He'd prefer that, I'm sure!

Which explained why her pugnacious little jaw was sticking as far out as it could go when she cornered the fiend, still munching bread and sipping coffee.

I hope he chokes, she thought, but the words that came out were all sweetness. 'Your mother thinks you ought to stay a little longer, Steady. There seems to be a crowd down at your place.'

'Spilled the beans, did she?' That big grin again.

It's no use, man, she thought. Now that I know what you're up to, you're wasting grins on me. I've got your number, buster!

'I don't know what you mean,' she answered. 'She was—worried about your health, that's all.' And isn't that strange? His mother didn't ask a single question about his health! 'And this mist is getting heavier. I think you'd better come on into the living-room now.'

'I don't think so,' he said blandly, 'and I'm the patient.'

'I *do* think so,' she said as she drained her coffee-mug. 'And *I'm* the nurse!'

From time to time during the afternoon, Alison peeped into the living-room. When lunch was served, Juanita had come in to join Steady. The pair had eaten together, played around the room together, and thoroughly enjoyed each other. At three, just to demonstrate the power of her office, Alison went in to spoil their fun.

'I can't help it, Mr Colson,' she said. 'You're here under the doctor's orders. The prescription was rest. That bump on your head isn't doing any better. We'll have to put an ice-pack on it.'

'Are you sure?' He didn't sound too happy about the prescription. And neither am I, Alison thought uneasily. It might do him some good. It can't possibly do him any harm. And how else am I going to keep a grown man in one place for the rest of the day? So she strapped the ungainly ice-pack on his head, using a couple of acres of bandages to hold it—or him—in place.

For perhaps fifteen minutes, she noticed, her interruption put a damper on the little party. Smiling to herself, Alison went down the hall to where baby Conchita was waiting, and mixed play with massage, because the rain made things too cool, even in South Texas, for a trip down to the pool. That work done, she came back up to the living-room and peeped in again.

It was ridiculous, the scene in front of her. Juanita was cuddled up in Steady's lap. The child spoke Spanish and Quiché; the man spoke only English. Yet despite this barrier, he was telling her a story—complete with gestures—and she was enjoying every minute of it!

On her next trip by the living-room door, some twenty minutes later, she found that the girl was fast asleep, sprawled across his arms, while Steady was leaning back against the chair, fast asleep himself! The bandages had slipped to one side, and the ice-pack was on the floor. And let that teach you a lesson, Alison Springer, she lectured herself. Never interfere between a man and his girl! There was a touch of bitter warmth to the idea—a man and his girl. She swallowed hard and went back to the kitchen.

GET 4 BOOKS

Return this card, and we'll send you 4 brand-new Harlequin Presents® novels, absolutely FREE! We'll even pay the postage both ways!

We're making you this offer to introduce you to the benefits of the Harlequin Reader Service®: free home delivery of brand-new romance novels, months before they're available in stores, AND at a savings of 26¢ apiece compared to the cover price!

Accepting these 4 free books places you under no obligation to continue. You may cancel at any time, even just after receiving your free shipment. If you do not cancel, every month we'll send 6 more Harlequin Presents novels, and bill you just $2.24* apiece–that's all!

Get 4 Books FREE

SEE BACK OF CARD FOR DETAILS

'If he gonna stay long, we need more food,' Carmen, her usually smiling face about as glum as it could get, registered her protest.

'I don't see why,' Alison answered. 'We've plenty of lamb, and a pile of mutton—in fact the cold-locker is full of it.'

'Yeah, but he say he don't like sheep. Not in no form at all, he says.'

'Well, isn't that too bad?' Alison snapped. 'I don't have all the time in the world to dither with his little choices. If he doesn't like lamb, he can go home to his mother! He either eats what we serve, or—do you suppose the budget could stretch to a side of beef?'

'Don't suppose,' Carmen answered. 'We down to a few pennies this week, *linda*. We don't get another cheque from the slaughterhouse until the end of the month, no?'

'Well, then, he's out of luck,' Alison said, thinking, And why am I so dispirited about it? He means less than nothing to me! If his stomach can't take it he can always go home and sleep in the barn! She thought back to the scene in the living-room. Little Juanita, cuddled up in a cute little ball, her jet-black hair strewn around her face; Steady Colson, his plain solid face, all planes and furrows, looking more relaxed than she had ever known before, his hair all awry, that absurd little bump on his nose etched prominently in silhouette. Why should he tug at my heart like that? Now if he were Fernando Lamas, or some good-looking man, it might be different. But he's not!

'Linda?'

Alison snapped out of her dream. Carmen, asking for the third time, was grinning at her. 'What? I—must have been thinking about something else.'

'Listen, *linda*. Why don't we do the way people in the villages do?'

'Sure. What's that?'

'*Oye, linda*. You don't act like this before *he* come!'

'Please, Carmen,' she pleaded. 'Whatever I'm doing different, it's got nothing to do with that big hunk of flesh in my living-room. Nothing! Ya'hear?'

'I hear.' But the Guatemalan woman was laughing at her. 'Look,' she continued. 'In the village, you want one thing but got another, you find someone who wants to trade with you, no? So here we are, up on the hill, with plenty lamb, mutton. Chops, steaks, roasts. Down in the valley is the Harrison spread. What they got? Beef, I betcha. Plenty beef, all kinds. You think they got a nice lamb chop? Never.'

'When you're right, you're right,' Alison sighed. 'I never would have thought of it. But, honestly, Carmen, I couldn't call them up and propose a trade. I just couldn't. I wouldn't want Mrs Colson to think I was pampering her no-good son!'

'You don't gotta,' Carmen replied. 'Mrs Colson a nice old lady, but she don't keep the house or cook the meals. They gotta cook.'

Alison swung around and stared at the little lady. 'How in the world do you know that?' she asked in astonishment. 'You haven't been down there since the Colsons moved in. How in the world——'

'Hey, I know,' Carmen repeated. 'They got one nice Mexican cook. Little old lady with six grandsons. You want I gonna call her, make a trade? Pablo be in off the range in ten—fifteen minutes?'

'I——' Alison stammered and then swallowed hard. 'Carmen Hernandez, we're equal partners around here. I can't give you any orders. *I* am certainly not going to call the Colson ranch and beg for some beef. You understand?'

'*Comprendo.*' The smile that went with the words was fulsome. That night they had steak for supper.

'That was a wonderful meal,' Steady said as he pushed his chair back from the table. 'That beef almost melted in my mouth. The first steak I've ever had that could be cut with a fork! I wonder why I can't get that sort of stuff down at my own place?'

Alison was taking a final sip from her coffee-cup. She almost drowned herself by pouring the liquid down the wrong pipe. 'I didn't think it was all that good,' Harriet Glebe said. The blonde had come zooming up to the house in a red Porsche at about five o'clock, prepared to spend as much time as required to snatch her fiancé from the hands of the infidels.

He reached over and patted Harriet's trembling hand. 'Had a hard day at the office?' he asked.

She seized on the topic avidly and ran away with the conversation. 'Terrible,' she said. 'I never knew there would be so much complication. Schedules, intelligence reports, administrative support—Steady, you wouldn't believe how complicated its getting to be. We'll concentrate in the city, of course, and—oh, lord, I shouldn't be talking here, should I?'

'I don't see why not.' Steady, his cheerful voice banishing all the shadows, waved a hand around the group. 'Nobody here but good American citizens, you know.'

'No, I don't know,' Harriet responded. 'It's getting so you don't know whom you can trust. Considering the Chicanos, the Indios, the Blacks, and the Anglos, I thought at least we could trust the latter. That's what I told the mayor this afternoon. But now I'm not so sure!'

'And did he laugh?' Alison asked.

'Why—how did you know?' Harriet looked across the table as if she suspected Alison had bugged her office.

'Because *he's* a Chicano,' Alison replied. The blonde's face turned red and her fists clenched on the edge of the table.

'Don't have no dessert tonight,' Carmen announced, getting up from the table. 'I do the dishes, and Pablo, he take the children down to our own apartment, Miss Allie?'

'No, you made the whole meal, Carmen. You and Pablo go ahead. It's almost seven o'clock, and you'll miss your favourite TV programme. I'll do the dishes and clean up, and Miss Glebe can talk to her—to Steady. *Vamos.*'

The little family gathered itself together. Juanita refused to leave without a kiss from Steady, and Harriet fumed all the more as every moment passed. When they had all gone, she said, 'I really hate to eat with the servants. Especially Chicanos. Well, you go out in the living-room, Steady. I'm going to help Alison with the dishes!'

It was hard to tell who was most affected by the statement. Colson's eyes bulged, as if he were hearing Gabriel's final summons. Alison, who had started up, sank back in her chair. 'You'll help with the dishes?' she repeated.

'Why, of course.' Miss Glebe was doing her cheerful best, and almost succeeding. 'I've washed many a dish in my life. My mother insisted that all us girls learn to handle servants and a house, you know. I can't think how often that training has done me good. Come along, now—I may call you Alison, may I? You do have aprons?'

Alison stumbled to her feet. The leopard had lost her spots? It hardly seemed possible. Just don't turn your back on her when she's working on the carving knives! she warned herself nervously. Steady pushed his chair back from the table. It scraped, adding a little more strain to Alison's already strained constitution.

'Go ahead,' Harriet said. 'I'll bring your coffee out in just a minute.' Sure go ahead—leave me alone in the kitchen with Harriet the Ripper! Besides murder, what else could she have in mind? How about telepathy? Alison asked herself. She squeezed her eyes shut and mentally screamed at him. 'Don't leave me alone. Don't!' When she opened her eyes again all she could see of Steady Colson was the back of him as he ambled out into the living-room. So much for sensitivity, she muttered under her breath.

'I'll dry,' Harriet said in her ear. Alison jumped, then recovered.

'We have a dish-washing machine,' she replied. 'Just scrape everything off and slide it into the—in there.'

'Well, I never expected you to have a machine in a dump like this,' Harriet continued. 'These walls look as if they haven't been decorated since 1898!'

'1864, more likely.' Alison, trying to conduct a defensive campaign without actually insulting the woman, wasn't having any luck. 'The War Between the States, you know.'

'I know.' Harriet offered an exaggerated sigh and promptly sat down on the tall kitchen-stool. 'Well, anyway, it gives us more time to talk.'

'How nice,' Alison managed to murmur. For some reason, her throat was dry, and the words were having trouble edging by her tonsils.

'Yes,' Harriet continued. 'Have you ever seen Huntsville?'

'Alabama? I went up there once to visit the Rocket Museum. When I was a little kid. My dad once worked up there, when Wernher von Braun was the chief designer.'

'Not Alabama!' Harriet snapped. 'Texas. That's where the State Penitentiary is located.'

'It must be exciting to know all that. I suppose that's something you studied in law school?'

'You might as well know, Alison, that the one thing I can't stand is an impertinent girl. I just can't stand them!'

'Luckily I'm a woman, and not a girl!' It's getting easier. All I have to do is maintain my cool and keep giving her the needle, Alison thought. And keep out of scratching distance! 'Just what was it you wanted to call my attention to in Huntsville?'

'It's a big, ugly place,' Harriet said. 'And the penalty for smuggling is twenty years to life. You'd hate it up there.'

'I suppose I would. But wasn't there something in the Constitution about a person being innocent until found guilty?'

'You needn't worry about that part. When we get through with this little sweep in the area, I intend to devote a large number of agents just to you, little Alison. Unless——'

'Aha! There's an *unless* in the woodwork.' Alison chortled. 'I'm glad of that. You had me worried. Just what is this "or else" you're threatening me with?'

Harriet raised both hands appealingly. Her tone changed from belligerence to sweetness. 'I thought perhaps we could reason this thing out, as mature adults, Alison.'

Alison, having stacked the dishwasher, slipped off her apron and hung it on a hook. 'That does sound nice. Go ahead and reason.'

'The problem, as you well know, is Stedman,' the other woman said. 'He's a very complex man, and I intend to marry him. Unfortunately, Stedman suffers severely from the roving eye. And he's equipped with a facile tongue. He and I are made for each other. We're both lawyers. My family is one of the leaders in the Anglo society in Texas. We're accustomed to wealth and position, both of us. We're of an age, Stedman and I. He's thirty-two, and I'm—er—thirty, you know.'

Do I know that? It sounded as if life had skipped a cog or two, Alison thought. But who cares about four or five years, when it's between friends? 'And I'm only twenty-six,' she sighed. 'I feel like a child in present company.'

For a second Harriet's eyes flared, but she made an admirable recovery. 'Yes, well, you haven't lived in the mainstream the way Stedman and I have. You *are* very attractive, for a back-country child, of course. And I'm afraid for you.'

'Afraid for me?' Alison turned her back, scrubbing the table with a wet sponge, hoping that she could keep the giggles suppressed. 'Why?'

'Because, as I told you, Stedman has a roving eye. After we're married I'll have him properly under control, Alison, but until then...' Harriet shrugged her shoulders as if the task were too much prior to saying the vows. 'And I can't help but notice that he has his eye on you. Now, you've been very nice to him—and to Mrs Colson. I wouldn't want your friendship to be rewarded by seduction. Would you?'

Now there is really a sixty-four-dollar question, Alison thought. Would I mind being seduced by Steady Colson? Looking at it hypothetically, it made an interesting question. Afraid that her sense of humour was about to get away from her, Alison kicked her toe against a chair-rung. The pain brought her back to earth.

'No, I don't suppose I would want to be seduced,' she said. 'By Mr Colson or by anyone else, for that matter. The coffee's perked.'

Harriet stirred off her stool and patted down her three-hundred-dollar royal silk dress. 'Then I think we understand each other,' she said. 'I'm glad we've had this talk.'

'Yes, I'm glad, too,' Alison agreed. No, indeed, Princess Harriet. I didn't want him *before* we had this talk, and now you've given me a basketful of *other* reasons for not wanting him. You're a great advocate, Harriet Glebe. If I ever really need a persuasive lawyer, you're my woman! 'Now, shall we take the coffee through?'

Steady was back in his easy chair, pillow-wrapped, reading the paper. He looked up as they came in with the tray. 'Ah. Just what I need. You know, Alison, there's something funny about this paper. I don't quite place what it is.'

Alison knew without looking. 'Nothing important,' she advised him. 'It's just that it's last week's paper. We don't get delivery this far out in the country. I manage to pick up a local paper once or twice a week. Too much national and international news is bad for the digestion——'

'Isn't she a quaint child?' Harriet interrupted. 'We had a lovely chat, and came to some fine conclusions.'

'Did you really?' Colson dropped his paper and looked at the pair of them warily. 'Conclusions about what?'

'Oh, just girl-things. You wouldn't be interested. Now, I have an early call for tomorrow, and I still must confer with the—with some people over at your ranch, Steady, so I think I'll run along now.' She proffered a quick kiss. He apparently made no objection, but neither did he help, Allie thought as she watched the pair of them. If this was romance, they must be an upper-stratosphere couple! No kiss, no handshake for Alison. 'You just remember what I said,' Harriet told her as she shrugged into her raincoat and went out to her car.

'Now there,' Alison said speculatively, 'is a whole lot of woman!'

'I suppose so,' Steady replied. 'If you like them packaged that way. Now, me, when I latch on to a lady, I want some give to her, some soft tenderness.'

'Hey, I know just the girl for you.' Alison backed away from his outstretched arms. 'Ophelia Brown! She and I went to high school together. I hear tell she weighs in at two hundred and ten pounds. Now *there's* a girl who could be a real handful for you. Several handfuls—or is that handsful?'

'I suppose,' he said very slowly, 'that this means I don't get kissed tonight, either.'

'I guess so,' she agreed. 'Drink your coffee. It's very expensive, and if you don't drink it while it's hot, it's spoiled. When everything else in the house gets wasted, we can feed it to the pigs. But coffee's a dead loss!'

'You know,' he said, 'I could get up out of this chair and run you down and get a real kiss—if I wanted to.'

'Think twice about it,' Alison Springer told him. 'You try, and if you don't have a concussion now, you'll have one *after* the performance. Go back to your paper. I have to go and say goodnight to the children.'

'And I'll come along with you,' he said as he hauled himself to his feet and followed her down the hall.

CHAPTER SIX

IT WAS a difficult night for Alison Springer. Her body betrayed her. After a hard ranch day, when normally she would be in bed and asleep long before midnight, on this night she tossed and turned and grumbled, and finally got up again. The skies had cleared. A pale quarter-moon was riding side-saddle out in the flatlands, and the rest of the house was quiet.

Clad in her long, cotton nightgown, barefoot, she paced the kitchen, the living-room, the empty west wing, and then strolled down to the room where the two children were asleep, their door half-open, the better to hear crying. There was none.

Each slept in her own little bed. Juanita was curled up around a huge teddy bear that once had cherished Alison herself. Baby Conchita was asleep on her stomach, her knees bunched up beneath her so that her little nappied bottom projected high above the blankets. She snored a little. Both were secure and safe and sleeping.

Alison sighed, watched for a moment, and went back up the hall. Why am I not asleep? she asked herself. Is it because I'm not secure, or I'm not safe? Is that why I'm not sleeping? What a ridiculous thought to have. What would Gran have said? I know. 'Come to bed with me,' the wise old lady would have said. But it was much too late for that. There was a world of difference between little girls and grown women.

So why am I hesitating in front of this particular door? Don't for the lord's sake tell me it's because this was Gran's room. Of course it was, but that's not important. Now it's Steady Colson's room! She didn't mean to push the door. She would have sworn on a stack of Bibles ten feet high! It was just that her hand was resting on the door, and she felt the need to shift her stance, all of which brought her weight over to *that* hand, and the door opened. It hadn't been latched correctly, of course!

But now, since it *had* opened, and nobody was to blame, why not look inside? I'm sure the Bible says something about Satan and *that* sort of reasoning, she told herself, but in she went.

The sliver of moon was bright enough to highlight the room. The big bed stood in the far corner, next to the front window, cast in shadows. But, having come that far, she hated to leave it at *that*! Three long strides carried her to the middle of the room, and common sense intervened. She halted, prepared to turn and steal away.

'Don't go yet.' The soft, low male voice came from the tangle of blankets in the shadows. Her breath whistled out as she gasped in fright, frozen in position.

'Come the rest of the way,' he invited.

'I—can't.' It was time to run, but her knees were quivering, and would just not obey.

'Come,' he repeated. The mass of semi-shapes changed. He was sitting up, holding one hand out into the moonbeams in her direction.

'I—no, I can't,' she whispered. It was *past* time to run. And I never should have come at all! she told herself fiercely.

'It must have been important, to bring you this far,' he coaxed.

'I don't remember,' she stammered. 'I must have been sleepwalking!'

'You remember. Don't lie. Come!' The springs on the old bed shifted uneasily. Her feet moved of their own volition towards the bed. Alison struggled, but seemed totally unable to stop her own legs. When her knees struck the bed she toppled over right on top of him.

'There we go,' he murmured in her ear. 'That wasn't so bad, was it?'

'I—shouldn't be here.' Her whole frame was shaking, and her voice reflected that. His arms came around her. Naked arms. Carefully, while one half of her mind told her insistently that she didn't want to know, she extended a hand upwards to the source of his voice. Fingers traced a path up through the soft, curly hair on his chest, up to his throat, up over his chin, and then back down slowly to his waist. She counted every rib as it pulsed in and out, felt the taut muscles of his stomach, and had a finger trapped at his navel. There was a delicious smell about him, an attractive mix of male and scent and lotion. And all the rest of him was naked, too! Naked, warm, and comforting.

'Don't fight it. You had to come,' he said.

It was that little teasing laugh that shocked her back to normality. A sudden flush of rage—at herself. A feeling of disgust. 'Hell, I'm some sort of a push-over, aren't I?' she muttered.

'Not at all, Alison.' A smooth, mesmerising voice, smothering her. It galvanised her into action. She kicked out against him, threw him off balance both physically and mentally, and tossed herself backwards to land with a thump on the boards of the old floor.

'Hey, you didn't have to do that.' The seductive voice had been replaced by anxiety. He must have been so sure of himself! she thought.

'Yes, I do have to,' she almost screamed at him as she scrambled to her feet and raced for the door. He made no attempt to follow. Bravado required some parting shot. 'You'll have to mark me down as the one who got away,' she said as she paused, one hand on the doorknob, the other clutching the torn neck of her nightgown.

'Temporarily,' he said cheerfully. 'It happens. There'll be plenty of other times.'

I'll be darned if there will be, she thought, but even in Quiché there were no proper words, either for her own stupidity or his cupidity. She ran down the hall, slammed her own door behind her, dived under the blankets, and shivered in shame for the rest of the night. All of which explained why she was huddled at the kitchen-table, nursing her second cup of coffee, when Carmen came in the next morning.

'No, I just couldn't sleep,' she replied as Carmen queried her. 'Something to do with the moon, or stuff like that.'

'You need a tonic,' practical Carmen said. 'That stuff you Gran leave on the shelf?'

'Not that,' Alison said in alarm. 'That stuff tastes like petrol!'

'So I make herbal tea. With a touch lemon, and a spoonful honey. I get it, *linda*.'

'I don't——' Alison started a protest, but knew that to refuse would insult her friend. I'm lucky I have a friend, she thought as she swallowed the words. Nothing could have been done without Pablo and Carmen. It had all worked so well for so many years, up until the moment that that crazy man got his foot in the door!

As if on cue, Steady Colson walked in. His rugged face was clean-shaven, his sandy hair wet and brushed, and he was wearing the new set of denims that his mother had sent up. Feeling like a hag, with her hair unbrushed and her shabby green robe barely hiding her nightgown, Alison shifted her chair away from him as he sat down.

'You sleep well?' Carmen asked.

'Never better.' He winked at Alison as he adjusted his chair. 'Can't think of anything more pleasant. Dreams, you know. I dream a lot.'

'Is so?' Carmen asked. 'Plenty things said in dreams. Maybe they come true.'

'It is to be fervently hoped for,' he replied, and the chuckle was barely hidden. Alison blushed and turned away from him. Carmen came back to the table bringing Alison her steaming cup of herbal tea, but in the moment of haste she put it down between the two of them, and Steady picked it up.

'Great day in the morning!' he roared as soon as he recovered from his choking fit. 'Somebody's trying to poison me!'

'What a charming idea,' Alison said, making no attempt to hide her bitterness. 'Maybe if you're feeling all that well you ought to go home.'

'*Linda!*' Carmen, six or seven years older than Alison, often thought of herself as the girl's mother. 'Manners, no!'

'I—I'm sorry,' she mumbled as she rescued her herbal tea. It tasted no better to her than it had to Steady, but at least she had been spared the surprise. 'It does taste abominable, doesn't it?'

'Not half as bad as that stuff you served the other night.' He grinned at her again as he cupped his fingers around the coffee-mug which Carmen had hurried along. 'But I'll tell you what we ought to do today.'

'I think you've got the wrong girl,' Alison muttered. 'I don't care much for men telling me what I ought to do!'

'Just men? Or are women included, too?'

'Don't try to psychoanalyse me,' she told him. 'If I were really a man-hater that *would* have been poison, not just herbal tea! But there are *some* men,' she admitted, 'who affect me the wrong way. And there's nothing they can do to change my opinion!'

'Thank the lord there aren't any of that type around these parts,' he said expansively. 'Now, what I thought we ought to do is kill three or four birds with one stone. I need to get some more clothes. You would certainly want to check up on that crowd at my house——'

'Why in the world would I want to do that?' she interrupted.

'Two reasons,' he said. 'If you're just a nice ordinary girl being put upon by some chauvinistic man, you'd want to check the truth of the story about there being no room at my inn. And if, on the other hand, you're actually the chief of a crew of smugglers, you'd want to hear all the plans of this raiding party. How's that?'

'That's terrible,' Alison said. 'And so's this tea, Carmen. Is there any more coffee left?'

'Plenty, *linda*.' Carmen flashed her gold tooth. A grin for him, and a shake of the head for her. 'Don't let him get your lamb.'

'Goat,' Alison corrected absent-mindedly. 'Don't let him get your goat.'

'Don't got goats,' Carmen reminded her. 'Have to be lamb. Maybe we ought to have goat. Or maybe even a couple cows? Don't I tell you before, we all need milk!'

'All right, all right, don't nag me,' Alison sighed. 'Go ahead, Mr Colson. Tell me the rest of your plan.'

'Why, we'll just ride down to my ranch,' he resumed. 'That mare out in the barn *will* carry you? Close your mouth, Alison, it's not good manners to gape at the breakfast-table.'

'Some day,' she threatened. 'Some day you'll get just what you deserve!'

'I pray for it every day,' he sighed. 'And so we'll ride down to my ranch and visit my mother. She'll love that. Hospitality. Texas hospitality. Maybe we can lay on a barbecue?'

'I can't spare the time,' Alison grumbled. 'I have to give Conchita her exercises.'

'That's another thought,' he added. 'Where are the children, Carmen?'

'Eh? *Los niños?* They go with their father to the barn. You know, to feed the chickens, the ducks, to turn the horses out in the corral. Like that.'

'Then how about if Alison and I were to ride down this morning and arrange things, and you and Pablo and the kids can come down for a barbecue lunch? Say about one o'clock?'

'*Bueno.*' Carmen turned anxiously towards Alison. 'And you, *linda?*'

'Oh, I don't mind people talking over my head,' Alison answered, and was instantly contrite. 'Of course we can all go, love. It will be a treat for everybody.' The glare she directed in Steady's direction finished the statement: even if the treat is at the hands of this monstrous creature!

He read the message very well, and for just one second there was a flash of doubt and concern in his eyes, which he instantly quelled. 'So, if that's all settled, why don't you go get dressed, little lady? My mother is old-fashioned. I doubt if she would appreciate your coming in your nightgown.'

Alison was still sputtering as they came around the curve of the Farm-to-Market Road above the Colson spread. Sputtering with laughter. He was a man of infinite humour, peopling the wide empty spaces with dreams so real that she could almost see his vision. It wasn't until the trip was almost ended that she analysed his humour. There was no cutting edge; almost every joke he made used himself as the butt. And puns ran rampant; a listener had to be sharply attentive or miss half the fun. And besides that, he was a fine figure of a man, sitting in the saddle of his palomino like a real 'cowpoke' instead of a lawyer.

'Samson here, he just doesn't care for this ambling along,' he told her as the horse pranced for a few steps. 'He was trained for the movies, by an old stunt man who worked for Republic Studios—remember them?'

'Vaguely,' Alison said. 'Long before my time. Cowboys and Indians, and like that?' Princess, her dappled grey mare, had long since given up the gallop and the nervous prance. A nice steady walk was Princess's idea of a good time!

'And like that,' he agreed. 'That's what convinced me I wanted to be a rancher. Roy Rogers, the Lone Ranger, Gene Autrey. When I was in high school I used to save all my money to buy cassettes of those movies.'

'And you never thought you might go bust as a rancher?'

'I don't figure to,' he replied. 'One thing I've learned—if you've got enough money, you can afford to hire brains. And if I do go broke, I'll just scout around for some outrageous law case to defend—like you, being arrested for smuggling.'

'I wish you wouldn't keep harping on that subject,' she objected. 'I'm getting a nervous feeling about it. Besides, I don't have enough money to rent your briefcase, never mind your brain.'

'Not to worry.' He kneed his horse over beside her and pulled up. His leg was rubbing against hers, and for some stupid reason she didn't want to move away. 'I have a sliding scale of fees,' he said with a pseudo-leer. 'And for a good-looking lady——'

'Which I'm not,' she said, kicking Princess into a faster walk. Her mare grunted a protest, but moved off.

'Which, as the lady says, she is not,' he murmured. Alison kicked her mare one more time. Princess broke into a reluctant trot. And since I'm sure I don't want him to seduce me, Alison thought, why do I feel so darn lonely the moment I move away from him?

She made a coaxing noise, leaning forward close to her mare's ear, and so was in front of him as they entered the cleared yard in front of the Colson house. Unlike her own spread, this homestead had been lovingly cared for. The house glistened in new paint; the open yard in front of it was grass-covered, with a U-shaped dirt drive for entry. More than a dozen unmarked cars were parked in cluttered disorder along the drive.

'It *does* look a little crowded,' Alison admitted as he reined in beside her.

'Oh, ye of little faith.' He chuckled. 'C'mon. Mom will be over the moon to see you.'

'Don't count on it,' Alison replied. Her last reception by his mother had been—strange—to say the least. But there was no need for immediate worry. Her second encounter was to be postponed. Steady swung down from his saddle and came over to help her. She had no need, but it was such a nice offer that she swung both feet out of their stirrups, brought her right leg over the pommel of the saddle, and slid down into his arms. All very tasty, she thought, as she slid down the length of him. It was a small disappointment when her feet reached the ground and he let go.

'Hey, here's the very man we're looking for!

Both Steady and Alison looked up at the screened porch. Men were boiling out of the house like bees from an aroused hive. At a distance they all seemed to be disquietingly the same. Tall, healthy, young, dressed in three-piece suits, and wearing their own hair. Or so Alison thought. She giggled. Steady Colson, still holding her arm, shook it gently.

'No improprieties,' he murmured in her ear. 'This is the dignity of the law!' The introductions began. There were twelve of them, and they lined up to be presented. All Alison could think of was a roll-call for the Twelve Disciples. Names went completely over her head. As her hand was variously squeezed and teased, her ear was assaulted by, 'Agent—— Agent—— FBI Agent—— Special Agent, Treasury Department——' and so on down the list, until it seemed that every Agency of the Federal Government had representation.

'And this is the lady your mother swears by?' Agent Simpson asked after his third introduction.

'Swears at, more likely,' Alison said primly.

'No, no,' Agent Simpson insisted. 'You run a ranch, support a couple with kids, run a business enterprise in the city—no, indeed, Mrs Colson has nothing but high praise of you. She says you're a complete *ranchera*. Did I pronounce that right?'

Alison nodded and grinned. Mrs Colson likes me? she mused. Well, probably because I'm not out to marry her only begotten son. Let's see if I can't keep it on that level! 'Oh, there's nothing wrong with your pronunciation,' she said, 'but there *is* a language problem.'

'Oh? *Ranchera* doesn't mean a female rancher?'

'No, that's exactly what it means—in Spanish. But language and culture often diverge, you know. Let me explain. A *ranchero* is a big male boss, the owner of a spread. *Ranchera* is the Spanish for a female who holds the same position.' She took a deep breath and looked around the circle of proud male faces.

'But no Texas male,' she continued with a grin, 'would ever admit that a woman is capable of running a spread. Therefore, *ranchera*, while being linguistically correct, is actually an impossibility. It follows then that the word is never used!'

'Are you sure you're not just another lawyer?' Mr Simpson asked suspiciously.

'Honest to Gawd,' she returned in her best Texas drawl.

'Now that that's settled, how about our problem?' one of the men in the back of the crowd asked. He passed forward, over the heads of the others, a folded section of the *San Antonio Express News*. Simpson, who seemed to be acting as the *de facto* leader, held it up for Steady to see. Alison, peeping around his shoulders, managed a look at the picture. Harriet Glebe was on display in her office, all business. 'What's the story?' Steady asked.

'*Your* lady friend——' Simpson took a second to savour the first word '—seems to be shooting off her mouth. Listen to this.' He quoted from the sub-headline. '"DA announces Federal Task Force Gathers."' He gave Steady a disgusted look and slapped the newspaper into

the pit of his stomach. 'Maybe if she had announce-
ments printed we could mail them to all our suspects and
invite them to give themselves up!'

'Hmm,' Steady muttered as he read the story. A quick
reading, too, Alison noted. He must be a speed-reader.
And why not? He was a speed-schemer, and evidently
a speed-lover, so why not? 'Yes, that's pretty serious,'
Colson told them after he had finished. 'I have only one
minor thought. Harriet Glebe has been a friend of my
family for years. I'm sure that she must have a perfectly
valid reason for a public statement. Now, how about
giving me time to say hello to my mother?'

He put his arm around Alison's shoulders as if to make
some point, and the crowd separated and let them go
on into the house. Mrs Colson was waiting in the living-
room. 'Oh, lord, Steady, are they ever mad!' she said.

He set Alison aside gently and gave his mother a big
hug. 'Hi, Ma. We've come for that Texas barbecue.' And
how about that? Alison thought. Just an offhand idea
up at my place, but all of a sudden his mother knows
all about it! He's as smooth as a snake's belly, but he
keeps forgetting his lines!

His mother gave him a wry look and turned to Alison.
'What we know about Texas barbecues,' she said, 'you
could put in a thimble and still have room enough left
over for your finger. What we're going to have is an
Oklahoma barbecue!'

'Just as long as the sauce is—lively,' Alison replied.
'Nothing else matters. Use some Jalapeño peppers. Not
too many, or you'll burn the insides of their mouths. It
gives a sort of flavour that we call, down in these parts,
Tex-Mex.'

'Ah! I knew you would know,' Mrs Colson said and
rushed out of the room to relay orders to her foreman.

'What did I tell you?' Steady asked. 'Alison Springer can do no wrong! At least, that's what my mother thinks.' Before Allie could escape, he gathered her up in his arms and grinned down at her. But whatever he had had in mind was interrupted by his mother's return.

'I'm sorry, Alison,' she apologised. 'But Matt is an Oklahoman, too. He says he wouldn't dare put those— Jalapeño peppers—in his sauce. So I told him you would come out and oversee the affair.'

'I don't mind,' Alison agreed, forcing herself to step away from Steady. 'Of course, it will require a little muscle-power.'

'That's what Steady is for,' his mother said. 'Go along, Stedman, and do what the nice lady tells you!'

'Nice lady,' he murmured in her ear as they went out of the back door. His hand reached for her hip. She slapped it down and danced away from him. The area behind the house was in an uproar. Two narrow troughs had been dug in the ground. Charcoal gleamed golden warm in each, and two beef cattle had been slaughtered. The carcasses, pierced by steel, were suspended over the charcoal, some three feet above the coals. Manpower was at the cranks at each end, slowly turning them.

Matt turned out to be a grizzled old Indian, Matthew Swift Eagle, a Cherokee from the Wester Nation. 'I been barbecuin' for fifty years,' he said. 'I put Jalapeño peppers in this sauce, and those tenderfeet are gonna go right through the roof!'

'Just a little, Matt,' Alison pleaded. 'Two or three— or four?'

'The peppers is on the table,' he said with a gesture. 'The sauce is in that drum by the fire. You put them in, you get the blame.'

'Right.' Armed with apron and a sharp knife, Alison carved the peppers into bits, then forced them through a sieve before adding them to the bubbling sauce. She handed Colson the big wooden paddle. 'Stir,' she commanded.

Steady Colson stripped off his shirt, picked up the paddle, and stirred as if his life depended on it. Alison stood behind him, admiring the thrust and movement of those massive muscles. There was something so— sensual—about them. From neck to waist, he was all muscle. A gorgeous hunk, she told herself. Now, how come I've never been impressed before by male beefcake?

'Well?' Steady asked.

'I'm sorry,' she said. 'I guess I wasn't paying attention. What did you say?'

'I said I've been stirring for fifteen minutes, and——'

'I'm sorry. Let me taste.' She took one of the wooden spoons out of its rack, dipped up a little of the sauce, and blew on it. Moments later her tongue gently tasted. 'Holy murder!' she exclaimed. 'Something to drink— please!'

There was water handy. She doused the fire in her mouth and thanked him. 'Too hot?' he asked.

'Just right,' she gasped. 'It's just hot enough. Not hot- warm, I mean it's hot-hot!'

'Don't try to explain,' Colson said. 'I probably wouldn't understand, anyway. And here come the kids!' He abandoned his stirring paddle and ran. The two little girls were waiting, dressed in their Sunday best. Steady swept them both up in his arms and there were hugs all around. For everybody but me, Alison thought as she gave Matt directions about using the sauce to baste the meat. For just a moment she felt shut out of paradise.

It was Conchita who broke the mood. She wiggled until Steady set her down, and then set a wobbly path towards Alison. Allie kneeled down in the soft grass, held both arms wide open, and waited. The baby toppled over a couple of times, got up bravely, and finally wandered into safe haven, chirping some indistinguishable phrases to mix in with her hugs. As a reward, Alison kissed her little button nose and tickled her under her ribs.

'*Oye*,' Carmen said as she came up, out of breath. 'I chase this pair ten thousand miles—kilometres? Today they don't give me any peace at all, let me tell you.' She looked over Alison's shoulder at the barbecue pit and her face lit up. 'Nothin' I like better than eat somebody else's cooking! Pretty soon?'

'About a half-hour,' Matt, at her elbow, reported. 'We started things off about ten this morning. Gonna be nice and tender—and, with that sauce, hot!'

'Well, *Gracias a Dios*,' Carmen said. 'I get tired all this Anglo stuff, no? Bland. Is that the word, *linda*?'

'That's the word,' Alison confirmed. 'You want hot, you get hot. Today, anyway.' She looked down to find Juanita pulling at her skirt. 'Where did Steady go?'

Pablo, moving at his usually unhurried amble, joined them. 'That woman arrived,' he announced. 'That Glebe woman. She comes all smiles; everybody in the place glares at her; she says something nasty; Steady, he grabs her by the arm and tows her off to the library, I hear. They're still in there. Somebody's doing a lot of yelling. An' that's all I know.' He smiled down at Juanita and swung her up in his arms. The girl stared at him with those big, solemn black eyes, and then returned the smile, throwing her arms around his neck. The power of love, Alison told herself, and added her smile.

'Did you know, Pablo,' she said, 'you may be in the wrong trade? You'd make a heck of a good spy!'

'You'd better believe,' he muttered as he moved closer to her. 'I go up to the *cañón* before noon, *linda*. Just for a quick look. There are all sorts of strange footprints up there—they're not there yesterday, you understand. And way up in the hills, up behind Silhouette Rock, there is some *muchacho* with binoculars, studying me, studying the area. Tan suit or uniform he wears. I don't think he's too bright. He holds the binoculars so the sun shines on the glass. If I was to guess——'

'So guess,' she interjected.

'Sheriff's men,' he said. 'Watching our back door.'

'Sheriff's men? You're positive?'

'No, I'm not positive,' Pablo said. 'I just *think* so. After all, the Federal men are down here at the bar-becue. Looks to me the Sheriff didn't get invited to the eats. Maybe they don't get along, the Feds and the local people?'

It was a day of bright summer sunshine. Alison shud-dered despite the heat. Federal men at her front door, a dozen or more of them. Unknown watchers at her back door? Except for the Farm Road in front, and the mountain trail behind, there was just no other way to access the Springer spread. Or no other way to get out, for that matter.

She shrugged her shoulders. 'I don't know what to do, Pablo. Nothing—that seems to be the best answer. We are who we are, and they can't prove otherwise unless they catch us in the act. Enjoy. Eat. Drink.' Pablo nodded and moved away, leading the two children a safe distance from the open fires.

And to whom do I owe all this attention? Alison asked herself. Deputy Chase? He was like an old bulldog, and he had his teeth into Alison Springer. But he hardly qualified in the brain department. Would he think to bar her back door over the hills? Probably not. So then we came to Harriet Glebe. She had more than sufficient motive. Not only did she believe what the deputy reported, but she felt that Alison was some threat to her hold over Steady Colson. Add on to that another fact. District attorneys get elected to their jobs. The present incumbent, and his assistants, face a new election in the fall. So mix hatreds and official complaints and politics—could Harriet be behind it all? The only question in doubt was, did that woman have enough *savvy* about the hill-country to picket the back trail?

Someone was cutting strips off the barbecue. Someone else was piling plates with meat, potato salad, refried beans. One of those plates arrived in Alison's hands. She fumbled with it, her mind still miles away. What did she know about Harriet Glebe? Only what she had read in the Sunday issues of the *San Antonio Light*. The Glebe family was locally well known and politically powerful. Harriet was a cousin from Fort Worth, who had come to San Antonio directly out of law school some five years past. A star in the Anglo social community, she hardly ever appeared at Chicano functions. Ambitious, some said. But was she that bright?

Alison shook her head. There was only one brilliant new mind in the area, one capable of studying the terrain, the political scene, faster and more thoroughly than most who had lived here all their lives. One who was loosely associated with the law. Or maybe that was some sort of cover? One who was sheltering this big raiding party on his own ranch. One who——

'Why is it that I can see you're standing here, and yet I know you're miles away? Aren't you going to eat any of this wonderful barbecue?' Steady Colson interrupted her thoughts, brought her back to the hot Texas reality. Steady Colson, who, having handed her a full plate of food, was now studying her quizzically. Steady Colson—one who!

'Yes,' she stammered. 'I was about to—where's Harriet?'

'In the crowd somewhere.' He waved vaguely towards the crowd at the serving-table.

'I expect she's hungry,' Alison murmured. 'She works hard, I hear.'

'She'd better be hungry,' he replied. 'She's got a lot of crow to eat this afternoon. Why are you always trying to keep track of Harriet? Does something about her bother you?'

Alison fumbled. The trouble with barbecues was having to balance a full plate, a cold drink, and your dignity, all at the same time.

She didn't want to answer his question. Mostly because that answer had just slammed into her own brain. A double-barrelled answer. Alison Springer was falling in love with Stedman Colson! Stedman Colson was the man who——!

The idea was ridiculous, of course, and must be fought off, even if it required some physical action. Hit him? He looked too big to stand still for that, so she abandoned the idea, and instead made up a little sandwich from the sliced rolls and barbecue meat. One bite burned like fury. She gasped, spooned up some of the cold potato salad and sighed. 'Just right,' she said.

'That's what everybody says,' he replied. 'Liked it a lot myself. Wouldn't do for every day, but it's certainly a nice surprise. There's a lot to be said for Mexican food.' He had his own plate well in hand, Alison noted with some chagrin. Something just had to be done to bring him down to the common level.

'It's not Mexican food,' she corrected. 'That's different. This is Tex-Mex food, a blending of both cultures.'

'Yes, ma'am,' he said. If she hadn't looked up at just that moment she might have thought him apologetic. But that big grin banished all such thought. No doubt about it, she thought, he's the man! And how in the name of all God's green earth could I be falling in love with the bad guy?

'You ought to be wearing a black hat,' she muttered.

'What? I didn't quite hear you?'

'I said,' she yelled at him, 'I have to move. I don't want to have that black cat walk across in front of me.'

'Oh, superstitious!' His laugh stifled the nearby conversation as other couples turned to watch them. 'I don't see any black cat.'

'He just ducked around the corner of the house,' she lied. Well, it wasn't *much* of a lie. Every ranch kept a brood of working cats around. One or more of them were *bound* to be black. She spooned up some of the refried beans. 'Eat,' she urged him. Do anything, but stop asking me all these questions!

When she looked up at him again he was doing just that. Eating, and watching her. The grin had disappeared. His head was cocked to one side as he studied her. He looked to be the final enigma; a very positive man faced with a doubt and a puzzle, and not sure what to do next.

And now's the time to test him, Alison thought. She phrased and rephrased the question a half-dozen times before asking, 'When is the great raid going to be?'

He had a mouthful of salad. His teeth continued to grind away until he had swallowed it all. 'Oh, tonight or tomorrow night, I guess.' His facial expression changed not a bit. He answered as if she had enquired about the next air flight to Dallas. After which, his little plastic spoon renewed its attack on the refried beans.

CHAPTER SEVEN

IT MIGHT have been the longest lunch Alison had ever attended. The barbecue was ready by one o'clock. They ate until three. The children both fell asleep at two-thirty, worn out by the exertion. Being the only infants in a crowd of fifteen men, all of whom had left families behind them, they overwhelmed the girls with offers of games and admiration. Pablo and Carmen packed them both up in the van and trundled them out of the Colson ranch by three o'clock.

'And I think the rest of you heroes ought to get in a little sack-time,' Steady Colson suggested. 'If you're going to be up all night, you need your beauty sleep.' Most of the agents agreed, disappearing one at a time until finally only the Colsons, Alison, a pair of ranch-hands, and Harriet Glebe were left.

'You should just let the fire-pits cool by themselves,' Alison advised Abigail Colson. 'It looks as if you've cooked three times more than you needed. The re-mainder of the meat should be cut and packed, along with the salads and stuff. Do you intend to store it all?'

'Yes, indeed,' Abigail said. 'My son, the lawyer here, came up with a fine idea. We're packing up all the left-overs, and we're going to have a left-over party tomorrow.'

'Looking at what's left,' Alison commented, 'it could be a running feast—good for a week, at least.'

'I don't think so,' Steady replied. 'This party will be held down in Brackenridge Park tomorrow, and we're

128

inviting anyone with an appetite and no money to come and participate.'

'Well,' Alison gasped in admiration, all her doubts temporarily forgotten. 'Stedman Colson, your stock just went up ten points in my estimation. What a lovely idea.'

'If that's what it takes, we'll have a party once a week for a year,' he said, grinning down at her.

'Stedman?' Harriet Glebe came up to him and laid a hand on his arm. 'You said you were going to share with me tonight. Don't you think you might need a little rest also?'

'I hadn't thought about that,' he said. 'I suspect you're right. This should be a strenuous evening, shouldn't it? We still have a couple of couches free in the study. Why don't you go along? I have something I need to tell Alison, and I'll be right with you.'

Surprisingly, Harriet agreed. As she walked by Alison, she muttered, 'Don't forget what I told you.' But Allie, whose emotions had been up and down like a roller-coaster all afternoon, was on the high side again. A moment after Harriet went into the house, Steady Colson came over to her.

'Alison?' he said, and then repeated himself. 'Alison!'

'Hmm?' she responded happily. His arms came around her, holding her loosely in front of him. He wasn't displaying his grin; now it was only a gentle half-smile, perched on one side of his mouth as his eyes blazed at her.

'Alison, Alison, Alison,' he murmured, pulling her closer. The kitchen door banged behind his mother as she came out on to the rear patio.

'Well,' Abigail Colson said after a moment of silence, 'Don't just stand there, do something.'

Steady Colson leaned over and kissed Alison.

There were times in every woman's life that stuck out in memory. And this will be one of mine, Alison told herself. Ranked up there with her first pony, her graduation from nursing school, Gran's death. It wasn't a wild kiss of passion and desert sand. Although Alison read her share of romances, she didn't expect that.

It was, rather, a kiss of warmth and love and comfort. All the way from her lips down to her toes, curling in her sandals. A kiss of cherishing and kindness and tenderness. Of laughter and care and affection. Of absolution and need and protection.

'I didn't mean to startle you so much.' His voice bespoke anxiety, as if he were still not sure of her.

'You didn't,' she said. 'I liked that. But didn't you have some sort of appointment with Harriet?'

'Why, yes, I believe I did.' That broad grin was back again. He tipped his stetson to her and wandered off towards the kitchen door. She watched his back as he moved. Not exactly graceful, perhaps, as he himself was not exactly handsome. But there was something there, as if he carried a sign which said, 'Here I come, stand in my way to your peril!' Alison chuckled at the idea, and fell back into her reverie. He was a man who—there was the rub. A man who what?

Cautiously she felt around this question, her mind probing with a clarity it had not known for some days. A man who? A man who suddenly appeared—out of the clear blue sky, so to speak—and bought a ranch which he didn't need. For his mother? Doubtful.

A man who shared his world with an ambitious assistant in the county attorney's office. A girl who wanted him, of course. But a girl who might well want something else—Alison Springer's head!

A man who was so smooth that nothing ever stuck to him. A big, broad man who hid himself behind a genial grin and a friendly manner, yet was known as the toughest lawyer west of the Rocky Mountains. A man who, as soon as he had got his ranch-house in order, invited a team of Federal agents to come and live in it. Why here?

And now the earlier information made more sense. A man who, having blocked the front entrance to the Springer ranch by having his own house on the only road, could also be the man who closed the back door by picketing that mountain road with the sheriff's officers! It began to add up.

The man who invented an excuse—a concussion, no less—so he could do his spying from inside the house of the prime suspect! But at that fork in the road Alison's conscience cried 'foul'. He didn't invent the concussion, idiot. You did that yourself. None of this scenario makes any sense unless Alison Springer is the prime suspect. And that doesn't make any sense at all. A suspect, yes, but our operation could be stuffed in an old paper bag along with two dozen oranges, and still leave room for *People* magazine!

But maybe he doesn't know that! Maybe his intelligence system isn't feeding him the right information. Maybe he just *thinks* that I'm the prime suspect! The whole thing was like a big crossword puzzle, and she had just slipped in the last piece. Of course that was the way it was!

All his attention to the children, all those black-market kisses, all those friendly smiles, all merely window-dressing so he could spy on us. What did they call it? Maintaining his cover! And she could hardly blame him for that. He was a law man. That was what 'lawyer' really meant. So, although he was entirely wrong in his conclusions, she couldn't really blame him for his methods, could she? Of course you can't, her conscience answered doubtfully. So why are you so damnably angry with him?

'I'll tell you why,' she muttered under her breath. 'Because *she* said something about "share with me" tonight, and he agreed. But then he couldn't wait, could he? He's in there right this minute, "sharing" with Harriet Glebe! What I ought to do is get a big axe and go in there and cut up their little game!'

'Alison?' The quiet voice at her side shocked her back to the present. Abigail Colson was at her side, a worried look on her face. 'Why, I heard you talking, Alison, and I came out, but there was nobody else around. And you sounded so fierce!'

Well, his mother can't help it if he's a bastard, Alison told herself, and then almost choked to death to get *that* thought straight! I *like* his mother. Maybe he gets his inclinations from his father?

'I'm sorry, Mrs Colson,' she apologised. 'I was daydreaming. I seem to have a number of bad habits. I dream in the daytime with my eyes wide open, and I walk in my sleep with my eyes closed, and——' She clamped her teeth on the rest of the words. *And I fall in love with the most unsuitable man!*

The pain was too much to bear. Her slender shoulders had borne the weight of responsibility for too long. The tears burst out in a torrent. She turned away from Abigail Colson, trying to hide them or stem them, with no good result.

'Here now, child,' Colson's mother said. 'There, there, now.'

With a wild sob Alison broke away from her and stumbled around the side of the house to the stable. Her mare had been unsaddled, and was cheerfully devouring Colson oats in one of the Colson stalls. Mrs Colson was coming up behind her. Burying her face in her kerchief, Alison headed for the road, running as fast as her breath would allow.

'Well, maybe you don't think so, but I do.' Alison was perched on the kitchen-stool at seven o'clock that night, her face pale, her eyes swollen and red. The bouts of anguish had passed. Worry still possessed her, but with it came the spirit to do something about it. Joan of Arc Springer was prepared to do her sainthood act!

'Ain't no reason to think we'd be raided,' Pablo insisted. 'Why us? Peanuts, that's what we are.'

'That may be.' Alison had decided to try her latest theory on someone else. 'But perhaps Steady Colson doesn't *know* that. I'm sure that Deputy Sheriff Chase thinks we're the centre of organised crime in Bexar County!'

'Yeah,' Pablo drawled. Thinking was not his best suit. Carmen did all that was necessary in their family; Pablo provided the muscle, the calm, the good humour, the love of children. 'Maybe. So what do we do next?'

'You and Carmen, you do nothing,' Alison said. 'I'm going into town. I have to meet up with Maria Santoso—but where? Down in Brackenridge Park, by the Big Spring. How would that be?'

'You watching too much TV,' Carmen interjected. 'One crazy idea, that one. Pitch dark, it is. No moon, plenty clouds. What kind woman walks in park on a nights like this?'

'An' besides,' Pablo volunteered, 'the fuzz run a patrol car through the park regularly at night.'

'So where?' Alison asked, discouraged. 'And how? If I leave here, someone is bound to follow me. If I call her on the phone—well, I think our telephone line is tapped. I tried to make a call an hour ago and there were strange echoes on the line!'

'Best place I know is where everyone else goes,' Carmen the Practical interrupted. 'What I hear on the radio? Big revival meeting tonight. Billy Gimble comes to Alamo Stadium! Preach the Word!'

'Oh, boy,' Alison sighed. 'That's great. We're going to invite one of San Antonio's fiercest Catholics to meet me at a Baptist revival?'

'Why not? What better cover?' Pablo asked. 'Besides, you drive the old truck down there and park, they have five—ten thousand people in the place, who's to know what you do? I can call Maria for you. I speak in Quiché, nobody knows what we say.'

'Including Maria,' Alison said. 'And besides, they trace the number you call, and right away they know who we're talking to.'

'So I don't call Maria,' he amended. 'I call Rafael Santandre. He speaks Quiché like a native——'

'Which he is,' Carmen interrupted.

Pablo gave her a disdainful look. 'And then Rafael, he calls Maria, and what do the police know? Nothing! Ten o'clock in the stadium?'

'Why not?' Alison shrugged her shoulders. There seemed hardly anything else to do, and Steady Colson's people were crowding in on her. This was the night for the big raid! Heaven help them! And what better place to ask for help than an evangelical meeting? 'Ten o'clock,' she agreed. 'By the Tuleta Drive entrance.'

A half-hour later Alison was ready, dressed in her most sombre style. Navy-blue slacks, ivory blouse, a grey blazer, and her sparkling russet hair in braids. 'Demure is what I want,' she told Carmen as she climbed into the truck.

'You got it,' Carmen replied. 'You look like some eighteen-year-old kid. Don't forget your Book.'

The old truck started on first cue, which augured well for the night. With headlights bright, she wheeled out on to the Farm Road and drove away at a modest thirty miles an hour. All the lights were on at the Colson spread. For minutes after she passed the house she kept an eye on the rear-view mirror, but nothing showed. Her luck held until she reached the junction of Route 2696.

Alison was doing all the correct things. She stopped at the sign, looked both ways up and down the empty road, and turned right. Almost immediately a pair of headlights sprang up from the darkness and trailed her. With grim concentration she ploughed along to the junction with Military Drive, the loop road that circled San Antonio. In this case the shortest route would be far from the quickest. She stayed on the loop until it edged southward. At the Austin Highway connector she turned into the city. Her fellow traveller stayed hard on her heels. At Hildebrande she left the highway and fumbled her way through the campus of Trinity University, and then into the crowded car parks.

The city traffic had delayed her pursuers. She locked the truck and scampered towards the walled stadium. The programme had already started; gospel music, amplified a hundred times, swelled through the night. And there, by the almost empty gate, Maria Santoso waited.

'I was followed,' Alison said, taking the older woman's arm. 'Duck into the crowd.'

Maria chuckled. 'If my bishop hears about this,' she teased. 'And I didn't even bring a veil!' Together they moved out into the stadium, found themselves a pair of seats in the middle of the crowd, and settled down.

'Now, what's the problem?' Maria asked.

Alison had been rehearsing her speech for hours. It flowed. All about the Federal team, her suspicion of Steady Colson, her fear of Harriet Glebe. 'I don't know where to turn next,' she concluded. 'We either have to make one big effort to dump all our packages, or we will have to pull in our heads and sit tight. Nobody moves, nothing changes. What do you think?'

'A terrible mess,' Maria said thoughtfully. 'But it has worked so well, so far, Alison. We must do nothing hysterically that would break the chain. You are the organiser, and the executive director. Me, I deal only with the committee—the supporters, no? What do you honestly think we should do?'

'Maybe two things,' Alison replied. 'Lay low. If they find out nothing, we can come up for air when they leave. The Federal Government are a funny bunch. They do great things with these sudden massive raids; but for the long haul, they can't handle it. Money, and more pressing cases keep interfering. So——' She took a deep breath, and for the first time noticed that the evangelist was praying 'for all sinners'. Which is something I could use a great deal of—prayer—she thought.

'Well, then, Maria.' Frightened little Alison Springer had put on her executive cap, and was prepared for action. 'You will pass the word, please, to all the stations. We pull in our ears and sit tight; if these raids uncover any one of our groups, the rest of us try separately to move all the goods on hand north, in any way we can. I will alert the Dallas committee as soon as I get back home.'

'Comprendo,' the elderly Chicana said. 'Everything will work out. Why not? God is on our side!'

'I hope so,' Alison said, but her mind was unsure.

'Why doubt it?' Maria asked. 'Is that not what the preacher says? Listen, how do we get out of here? Everyone is glued to the seats!'

'We don't,' Alison replied. 'We have to stay until the end, and leave with the crowd. I think there are some men still at the gates, waiting for me!'

'Listen, Alison. You have been right for so long, even though you are so young, you understand. But I can't help thinking. Maybe you are wrong about this man Colson? Why would the Federal Government pick on little people like us? It makes no sense, *linda.'*

'And I'm not wrong this time,' Alison whispered. 'He's a low-down, conniving, cheating—that man would do anything. You hear?'

'Shh,' Maria cautioned. 'Everybody in this section of the stadium can hear. So OK, he is a ratfink. Some day, when this is all over and we can laugh, I will ask Pedro to punch his face, no?'

'I—don't think it would help,' Alison said. 'He's a *big* ratfink. Maria, did the committee ever hire a helicopter to seed my ranch?'

Maria Santoso looked at her quizzically. 'Hire a helicopter? You must be mad, Alison. Why do you ask this?'

'Oh, it's nothing. Just a thought. Listen, here's the benediction. Move out with the crowd, but don't go out the same gate as I do.'

'They don't do it this way on Miami Vice,' Maria said. 'OK, *linda*, everything will be done just as you say. *Hasta la vista!*'

'Yes,' Alison returned. 'See you later.' Maria Santoso got up with the crowd and moved off. Allie remained seated until the other woman had a head start, and then moved along at the tail of the procession. *And there's another of his lies,* she told herself as she followed the amiable, chattering crowd, moving slowly. *He sent that helicopter!*

For twenty minutes Alison moved and stutter-stepped and paused and waited, until finally, with the car parks half-empty, she managed to get to her truck. The clouds had closed in, and a light mist was falling. It didn't make the deputy sheriff, standing beside her vehicle, any happier.

'Well, Miss Springer?' Deputy Chase said sarcastically.

'This *is* a surprise,' she replied. 'Working late, are we?'

'Made all your plans? Who did you come to meet?'

'Me? Plans? Yes, I suppose you're right,' Alison said, doing her best to sparkle in the face of fear. 'Long-term plans. We all have to go some time, so I thought I would come down and hear the Word.'

'Don't give me that,' Chase snapped. 'We know your habits, Alison Springer. You haven't been to church in over a year now!'

'That long? I hadn't kept track.' She tried her key in the door-lock. He shifted his position, blocking her movement. 'But if that's true,' Alison continued, 'it's about time I came, huh? Gran was a Southern Baptist, you know. She'd feel badly if she knew I had fallen from grace.'

'Bull!' The deputy's face glowed in the dark. Anger or beer? Alison thought. Probably anger! 'Listen, girlie——'

'Well, thank you,' Alison teased. 'I haven't been called that in years!'

'Tell me who you came here to meet!' he roared at her. A few couples, stragglers just finding their own cars, stopped to look at them.

'Why, Billy Gimble, of course.' Alison could hardly believe her own ears. Her voice sounded so sure, so calm, so authoritative. And here the deputy was grinding his teeth in a rage. 'Is that an offence you can arrest me for, Deputy?'

'If it was, you'd be in the *calaboose* so quick your head would spin,' he muttered. 'You done played with the law too long, Springer. Your number's up. Now get out of here!'

'When I'm ready,' she said staunchly. The door came open under her hand. She climbed up into the high seat, fastened her seat-belt, closed the door, and started the engine. And then sat there with the window wound down, defying Deputy Chase to do anything about it. He stood in the rain, watching her for more than a minute, and then he yelled at her.

'OK,' she replied. There was only so far you could push any man before he blew up. One of Gran's instructional lectures to a sixteen-year-old Alison. 'I'm ready!' The gears ground as she shifted poorly, but the old truck was accustomed to abuse, and took her safely out to the highway.

A pair of headlights appeared behind her as soon as she reached Hildebrand. She took the jagged turn north, instead of returning to the Austin Highway. A few miles of city traffic might test the skills of the follower. She

gave him—or them—a good test, but they kept up with
her until she turned into the Farm Road that led home,
and dropped off just before she passed the Colson
spread.

There was a night-light burning in her own kitchen
window as she drove up. Carmen and Pablo had long
since gone to bed. Alison slipped out of her wet things,
and into her shabby bathrobe. A cup of decaffeinated
coffee warmed her up as her mind rehearsed what she
next had to say. It must be couched in innocuous terms,
and delivered in a round-about manner. But the plans
had long been laid for the exigency. It was twelve o'clock
when she dialled the Dallas cut-out number and passed
her coded message into the larger unit's computer. And,
having done that, she walked down the hall to check on
the children, dried her hair and went to bed, leaving her
problems in more powerful hands than her own.

'Miss Alison! *Linda!*' Alison managed to prise one eye
open. The sun was shining, and Carmen was tugging at
her shoulder.

'What time is it?' she grumbled, letting that one eye
close again.

'Is eleven o'clock of the morning,' Carmen said,
adding a couple of extra shakes. 'He waits. In the living-
room, he waits.'

That brought both big green eyes open. She sat up in
bed. Carmen sounded so positive, so enthusiastic, and
Alison's mind was still drifting down the river of dreams.
'He waits?' she asked, puzzled. 'God? The sheriff?' And
who else do I have to be afraid of today?

'No, no,' the little Guatemalan woman bustled around
the room, pawing over Alison's few dresses. 'Hah. This
one.' *This one* turned out to be a blue little demure shirt-

waister in which Alison managed to appear on the right side of twenty-one.

'Who? For goodness' sake stop prancing around the room and tell me *who* waits in the living-room.'

'Is Mr Colson,' Carmen said. 'I didn't tell you before?'

Oh, lord, what a way to start a day, Alison groaned under her breath. All that lovely sunshine—and Steady Colson. Was this the way the French aristocrats felt when the guards came to take them to Madame Guillotine?

'Come on,' Carmen prompted. 'He plays with Juanita, but you can't expect a man to play with children all day.'

'And why not?' Alison asked as she stretched her feet to the floor. 'Pablo does.'

'*Aye, Dios mío,*' Carmen said, chuckling. 'Pablo—he is not like other men, no? He have seen what the world do to children, and he love them all.' She patted her way through the drawers of the heavy old bureau. 'An' wear the silk, no?'

'Wear the silk?' Alison was out of bed, reaching for her robe. 'You think he's going to inspect my underwear?'

'No, *linda*. Wear the silk. You feel—gooder?'

'Better,' Alison said.

'Yes. You feel better when you all dressed up, and when you feel better you act better. I think all night about him, *linda*. I think maybe he not so bad like you think! Nice man. He got some idea about you, too.'

'You bet he has,' Alison replied grimly. And I don't quite know his priorities, she added to herself. I'm not sure whether he wants to get me into his bed and then arrest me, or the other way around!

'So hurry,' Carmen insisted, pushing her down the hall towards the bathroom. 'Brush the teeth, comb the hair, fix the face. All that.'

Alison had no problem with the first part of the instruction. It was the 'all that' that slowed her up. It included facing herself in the mirror and building up her courage. What was that Harriet had said about the Texas state prison at Huntsville? Was it true that you went in through the gates and they never opened for you again? That no sunshine was allowed inside the building because it might make the prisoners feel good? And what would happen to Juanita and Conchita if all the adults were locked up? Dithering had become a full-time operation when Carmen knocked on the bathroom door. *'Linda,'* she shouted. *'Pronto!'*

Alison came out, shoulders squared, head held high, *pronto*! 'Don't worry,' she half whispered to Carmen as she went down the hall, 'I'm going to take all the blame.'

'Seguro—sure,' Carmen replied, completely puzzled.

As announced, Steady Colson was in the living-room sitting in Gran's old wooden rocking-chair, Juanita curled up in his lap. Why does he have to look so darn— paternal? Alison asked herself. He'll make some lucky girl the finest husband in the world. And what a sickening thought *that* was!

Steady looked up at her and grinned, unaware of the confusion he was causing in her mind. He tried to get up, child and all, but Alison waved him back to his chair. 'There's no need for that,' she told him. 'I—didn't expect you so early.'

One of his eyebrows went up. 'I wasn't sure you expected me at all,' he said. 'My mother told me you left the party yesterday in a very upset mood. I would have come, but I got myself involved in those raids late last night, and what with one thing and another I didn't get back to the ranch until four in the morning.'

'So then you came here immediately,' she stated. He shook his head slightly, and tickled the little girl.

'No, of course not,' he said. 'You forget the fiesta down at Brackenridge Park. I got up at seven to help move everything down there, and *then* I came directly here.'

'You're in some hurry to arrest me,' she said bitterly. A frown played across his face. And that's another thing, she told herself, he's getting more handsome all the time! It's not fair!

She watched as he set Juanita down on her feet and sent her in search of Carmen. And then, out of poorly focused eyes, she saw him come over to her and put a hand on each of her shoulders.

'I sometimes wish I knew what you were talking about,' he said. 'I don't have any powers to arrest anybody, and you're the last one in the world I'd want to arrest if I did have the power.'

'So then why did you come?'

His hands urged her forward. She went willingly, and turned her head so that her cheek rested on the soft wool of his sweater. One of his hands cupped the back of her neck, and then wandered through her loose hair.

'Maybe it's because I had to see you,' he murmured. 'Maybe I've lost control, little lady.' He sighed as he pressed her head gently into his chest, and then he chuckled. It broke the spell. 'And maybe it's because I need someone to organise this darn picnic,' he said. 'When I left, the kids were running wild!'

So it's a reprieve, she told herself. I'm to go along with him to get things straight in the park, and *then* he'll arrest me! Well, why not? I'm too tired to argue, and too weak to fight, and too scared to run away.

'All right,' she said, 'but I can't go dressed like this, and I haven't had breakfast, and—oh, to heck with it all. I'll be ready in ten minutes.'

And she was, but only because the old grandfather clock had stopped. Someone had forgotten to wind it. He had a car outside the door, a lush-looking thing, a sort of sinister two-door black bug that dared you to get in. He held the door open, and she made a graceful entrance, something not possible in demure little skirts. Now, dressed in trousers and blouse and sneakers, anything was possible.

'A sports coupé,' he said as he joined her. When the engine started she hardly heard it, although she could feel the car rock slightly under its power. 'An XR4i. I had a chance to nab one in Europe,' he added as they moved out towards the road.

'Of course,' she muttered. 'Doesn't everyone?'

'What?' He wound down the window and waved as they passed his house. 'My mother,' he said. 'I told her I'd wave if you'd agreed to come. Otherwise she would have been nominated, and she hates that sort of thing.'

'Yes, well, then I'm glad I could come,' she replied. 'It's not the sort of thing elderly ladies can do, you know, playing cowpoke to a herd of hungry kids.'

'That's great,' he said, 'but don't repeat it around my mother. She doesn't see herself as one of the rocking-chair generation. At least, not yet.' And that was about the gist of the conversation. Not for the life of her could Alison think of a single thing to say to this huge man, sitting at her side. This huge, handsome man.

Brackenridge Park was one of those anomalies of city life. In a place with more than three quarters of a million people, the park stretched across somewhat more than three hundred acres, a gift to the municipality at the turn of the century. In the natural stone caverns deep beneath the park bubbled the life-blood of Texas, pure spring water. Enough water to serve all of Bexar County and some of its neighbours, it spurted up to form the source of the San Antonio River, down which, for some fifteen miles, the locals could paddle their canoes, or drift—or watch the ducks while they picnicked, and hardly know they were in an urban area.

There were plenty of parents present. Working at full steam, Alison managed to get them organised, and catastrophe gradually shifted over to noisy enjoyment. 'See,' Steady commented as he came back for further instructions in the middle of the afternoon, 'all we needed was a leader.'

'All you needed was an organiser,' she chided him. 'Gran loved to hold barbecues. Not here in the park— that I find hard to believe. How did you get the licence?'

'I've got friends,' he said, and laughed at her as he did. 'So you've plenty of experience organising?'

'Barbecues,' she added firmly. 'Nothing else, just barbecues.'

'That's good to know, Alison. Did you know that you've got sauce on your nose?'

'Really? Wipe it off for me?' She leaned forward over the table, almost a little too far, but before she could fall those strong hands rescued her. 'Thanks,' she muttered as she tried to recover, but his hands were locked in place.

'The nose,' he said softly, and before she could protest he had shortened the distance between them by a nose, and kissed the spot where he had claimed the sauce lay! There was a sudden cheer from the mixed group of adults and children still waiting in line for fifth helpings. If there had been any sauce, it could not have been more red than Alison's cheeks.

'Not in public,' she muttered at him.

'It was good sauce,' he replied, licking his lips. 'But it can't last much longer. I do believe we're running out of food. And I'm glad of the progress.'

'What progress?' she snapped, more embarrassed than angry.

'Why, we've made tremendous progress,' he said very solemnly. 'Not more than two days ago it was "kiss me at your peril, Steady Colson." And look now—now it's "Don't kiss me in public!" I think that's really a step in the right direction. Now——' he came around the table, took her by the elbow, and hustled her off towards the car park.

'What are you doing?' She tried to shake herself free, but his grip was far too firm. Try a little artful persuasion, she told herself. 'We can't leave yet! There's food to be distributed, and cleaning up, and——'

'And Matt is going to take care of it all,' he said. 'Along with a committee of parents from the *barrio*. You and I have absolutely no reason to hang around any longer!'

'A lot you know,' she muttered. It wasn't much of an answer, but then she had never been good at snappy repartee.

'Yes, a lot I know,' he said as he pushed her into his sports car. 'And don't you forget it, lady. I've been to lots of schools and have degrees coming out my ears, and on the way I've managed to learn one or two things of some importance. Get in!'

'I'm in, I'm in,' she protested. The car engine roared, and then was instantly quiet as he closed his door and turned on the air-conditioning. Her elbow was a little sore, a victim of his enthusiasm. He followed the park road until he reached Broadway, and turned north. 'Where are you taking me?' she asked, very meekly indeed.

'You said "not in public",' he informed her. 'So we're going someplace where we can be private!'

And Alison Springer, who was not sure whether he intended seduction or arrest, or just more kisses, huddled in the corner of the seat and tried her best to look like a little brown mouse.

CHAPTER EIGHT

ALISON had another late morning. She had no idea what time she had arrived home. The previous day had ended with an emotional smash-up. Her bleary eyes read her alarm clock. Eleven in the morning! It had to be morning. The bright Texas sun was hard at work outside the windows, a pair of ravens were protesting a nesting area, and she could hear Carmen singing from the kitchen. Allie sat up in her bed, and a cool morning breeze played around her exposed breasts.

She grabbed for a sheet as she blushed from top to bottom! Naked, and in her own bed? That—monster—had driven them out of the city the evening before, and up Route 16 towards Helotes and Bandera. Out on the escarpment, at what looked to be a thousand miles from civilisation, he had parked the car in a bypass, facing south.

The lights of the city were spread out before them, and the towers and aircraft at Lackland, Kelly, Randolph, the old Air Force bases that circled the city, completed the picture.

'Private enough for you?' he asked.

Alison shivered. The weather wasn't all that cool, but his words were. 'I—don't understand what you want,' she whispered.

'You know what I want,' he insisted. 'The only question is—what am I doing? Alison, I don't know what the hell I'm up to. You've swept me off my feet. You're

148

an itch I can't scratch, and all I know at this exact moment is that I want you, girl. I want you!'

Had there ever been a more bald statement, she asked herself? Does he think I'm just going to lay back and think of England? 'No, I don't know,' she said angrily. 'And if I did, I wouldn't. Take me home!'

'Still on the edge of commitment?' His query had a taste of bitter anger behind it. 'Need to talk?'

Alison shook herself loose from her fears and sat up straight. He was, after all, only a man. 'I thought you would be up to your ears in guilty culprits,' she said scornfully. 'How come you're hanging around trying to make out with a back-country girl?'

'Alison Springer,' he said with a sigh, 'you are the damnedest tease I've ever met. After all this time, do we still have to debate?'

'All this time has hardly been two weeks,' she reminded him. 'And don't think your bit about not being involved with the Federal raids is going to cut any mustard with me. I know better.'

'I've told you a dozen times, I'm a trial lawyer!' he snapped. 'What does it take to get through to you?'

'A lot more times than a dozen,' she replied, her anger boiling over. 'Just because you've got a big car and a fancy ranch and—and—take me home.'

'All right,' he said. The anger was gone; a tinge of sadness had crept in. 'I never, ever guessed so badly before. OK, lady, "take me home" is the watchword. But I think at least you owe me a kiss!'

It didn't seem like a terrible price to pay. She sat still, turned her head slightly in his direction, and waited, expecting a brief peck at her exposed cheek. Instead, his arm came around her shoulders, and before she could fight or panic he had moved her over in the seat, to where her hip and his were touching. And then, in a smooth, practised move, he swung her up on the seat so that her legs extended towards the door, her head lay cradled on his chest, and his lips came down on hers.

Gently at first. As gentle as soft summer rain. Moist and warm and comforting, as it had been before. 'Why are you doing all this?' she whispered as they broke for breath.

'I don't know,' he muttered, and returned to the assault. But all the comfort had disappeared. His tongue teased at her mouth, his free hand wandered down to her hip, up across her ribcage. Sensation followed sensation. Sharp, coaxing feelings she had never known before as his fingers tangled with the buttons of her blouse, and cool air blew.

'No,' she muttered vaguely. His hand paused.

'No?' he repeated as he nibbled on the lobe of her ear.

'Oh, lord,' she replied. His hand took up the movement again. A brief twist, and her front-fastening bra floated away, taking with it all her moralities. His hand floated up the mound of firm flesh and established contact with the bronze tip that thrust itself upward in aching eagerness.

'Oh, lord,' she sighed. He shifted her weight, and those seeking lips came down the curve of her cheek, jumped off on to her neck, and found their way up to where the fingers had been. The reaction tugged at her very being. She squirmed closer to him, trying to satisfy her own passions. His lips continued the assault, while his hands struggled with the zip on her trousers. There was a tumult in her mind that could not be quieted. And suddenly that wandering hand had slipped down between her thighs, resting at the heart of her femininity. It seemed axiomatic that her thighs would spread to allow for the intrusion. Her mind was on fire, flaming to destruction, waiting, yet urging, and not really knowing what she urged.

Her eyes had been closed since the beginning. It was almost as if she were entrapped by an unknown being, and that couldn't be right! She forced one eye open. His head was down at her breast, his lips driving her to torment. Gasping, she brought up one hand, ran it through his hair, and around on to his perspiring forehead. And then he stopped.

'Hey,' he said. 'I'm too old for this. Doing it in the front seat of a car went out when I was eighteen. Come on, Alison, let's go find a motel.'

The words hit her in the face as if he had doused her with a pail of ice-water. She spent a moment seeking to control herself, and then turned on him. 'Let me go,' she said wearily. 'I don't know what you're thinking, but I don't do it. Not in a car, not in a motel, not any place. Take me home.'

She managed to sit up and swing her feet to the floor. Somehow her bra had disappeared. She fretted about it, and then buttoned her blouse. Two of the five silver buttons were missing. She shook her head in disgust— at herself as well as him. Out of the corner of her eyes she could see him, a vast shadow against the night skies, beating on the steering-wheel with one hand and staring straight ahead, having trouble with his breathing.

'So. It was *no* all along,' he said, sighing.

'I *said* no,' she whispered. 'I meant it. I know you must have a lot of experience with women. Good heavens, you turned me on in thirty seconds, and here I thought it could never happen. Well, it won't happen again, Mr Colson. Take me home, please.'

He did, of course, without another word, driving carefully at the speed limit, the exact opposite of his mood going *up* the escarpment. By the time they pulled up in front of the old Springer homestead the atmosphere inside the car could have suited the South Polar expedition.

'If it's worth anything to you,' he finally said as he opened her door for her, 'I'm really sorry, Alison. I got carried away.'

She stepped out of the car and patted down her clothes. 'If it's any consolation to you,' she offered, 'so did I. Goodbye, Mr Colson.'

'Goodbye?'

'Goodbye.' She walked slowly up the stairs, like an old woman just back from mountain climbing. The motor of his car didn't start up until long after the front door had slammed behind her.

Carmen came out of the kitchen at the sound of the door. *'Aye, Díos mio,'* the Guatemalan woman said. 'You look like you been in a fight, *linda*.'

'I was,' Alison replied sombrely as she headed for her bedroom. 'I lost.' She stripped, throwing her clothes in a heap in the corner, slipped into her robe, and went back to the bathroom, where she showered until the hot-water tank turned cold. She scrubbed and pummelled and scrubbed again, over every reachable inch. For some reason she felt dirty, and couldn't get clean. Finally, too chilled to stay longer in the shower, she dried herself off and went back to her bedroom, where she threw herself under the sheets, stark naked. Only to wake up late, and to hear little Juanita at her door...

The little girl, almost five now, her jet-black hair meticulously combed and parted, squealed in delight and ran across the room. Alison fumbled with her sheet, but still managed to catch the hurtling little form as it did a swan-dive in her direction.

'*Yo te amo,*' the child managed, in passable Spanish.

'I love you, too,' Alison assured her. Carmen stuck her head around the door-jamb.

'Ah, you awake, *linda*? The sheriff man is here again. I tell him to wait. He say he have a paper. I think to tell Pablo throw him on his ear out, but Pablo have go to the sheep. Jus' like a man, huh? Always somewheres else when I need him. You come?'

'I come,' Alison returned solemnly. It was no time for jokes. She could see that Carmen was worried—extremely worried. So Steady Colson had decided to take the coward's way out. Rather than coming to arrest her himself, he had sent the sheriff's man along. What a come-down! Carmen nodded, picked Juanita up, and went out. 'I tell him you come,' she called. 'Sooner or later, no?'

As it happened, it was *later*. Alison decided, as she forced herself out of bed, to go out in a blaze of glory. She showered leisurely, washed her hair and put it up, dressed in her silk undies, and slipped into her almost-new cornflower sun-dress. Another few minutes spent on make-up, and it was not the ragamuffin who came into the living-room, but a very poised and confident young landowner.

Deputy Chase had honoured her with his presence. It surprised Alison. With the Federal Task Force in the area acting as an up-to-the-minute law enforcement system, the local sheriff's department had been conspicuous by its absence. Now that the party was over, apparently, deputies were flooding the countryside. Besides Deputy Chase, bulking large in Gran's rocking-chair, there were two more cars parked outside, their lights flashing. None of it added up. And anything that didn't add up constituted a threat in Alison's mind.

'On your best behaviour?' Chase asked as he saw her come in.

'Always,' Alison said gravely. 'My Gran taught me to be a lady, Deputy. Do I understand you have another search warrant?'

'Not quite,' he replied, rising from the chair to hand her a paper. 'This is a subpoena. You are required to appear in the District Court at the time and place mentioned. How about that, Miss Alison?'

'You needed all these men to serve me this paper?' Alison gasped. 'What did you expect? Guerrilla attacks?'

'I don't take no chances with animals,' Deputy Chase said. 'An' you're not the only stop in my day, lady. Just see you pay attention to that summons. When she gets you on the witness-stand, under oath, believe me, you'll tell the truth for a change.'

'Well, I'm sure I will,' Alison answered. 'Who is she?'

'Miss Glebe. Harriet Glebe. She and I have had a long talk about you. She figures to hang you out to dry. Smart, mean lady, that one.' The sheriff chuckled as if he could foresee and enjoy Alison's court appearance. He gave her a jovial nod and headed out of the house.

'Am I supposed to stay at home until then?' she called after him. 'Or should I flee the country?'

'Don't make any difference, Miss Alison, 'cause we're going to catch you at it sooner or later.'

'I doubt it, Deputy,' she returned coolly. 'Since I'm not *doing* anything, I fail to see how you could catch me *at* anything.'

The man walked away, shaking his head. He barely made it back to his patrol car before the rains came again. Deputy Chase stuck his arm out of the window and shook his fist; Alison wasn't quite sure whether it was she or the Lord who was being threatened.

Soft, soaking rains they were this time, instead of the massive thunderheads. Alison went out to the porch and watched. Carmen came out of the kitchen to join her. Since the barbecue at the Colson place had brought no visitors up the hill, there was little for the two women to do except those odd-job items that seemed to forever bother women.

'What you watch?' the Guatemalan woman asked as she leaned over the porch rail.

'You wouldn't believe it if I told you.' Alison laughed. 'I'm watching the rain fall and the grass grow!'

'Is true,' Carmen giggled. 'Everything look green. That man is plenty smart. Who else would think to plant grass seeds from helichopper?'

'And dangerous,' Alison confirmed, suddenly solemn. 'He lied like a trooper about that whole affair!'

'Every man is dangerous, *linda*. All depends on how much smarter is the woman.'

'You can rule me out of the race, then,' Alison replied sadly. 'I couldn't compete with him on an odd Sunday after he'd been out drinking all Saturday night. I'm worried, Carmen. I haven't heard from Mrs Santoso. Not a word. And if Steady catches us in the middle of making a shipment, I'll be a dead duck.'

'Don't be discouraged. You do not remember. Smart man has the mind turn to mush when he watch a pretty girl like you!'

'Flattery will get you someplace,' Alison sighed, 'but I just don't know where. How are the children?'

'They do well.' Carmen laughed. 'Juanita is school-teacher today. She make the baby say the words. Pablo help them before he goes. They take words from the Bible. Man named Joshua. Funny name, no?'

'Old Hebraic,' Alison said. 'It means something like—whose salvation is in the Lord.'

'Have to go shopping,' Carmen said. 'Joshua? Just what what we need.' She giggled. 'A little salvation, no?' She was still laughing as she went back into the house.

It was the sort of day in ranching when practically nothing could be done outdoors. A 'make and mend' day, so to speak. But Alison, wandering through the house, could find very little to mend. The place gleamed with refurbishing already accomplished. Restlessly she paced the living-room, and it was there that Steady Colson finally trapped her.

'Ah, the invisible woman,' he said, coming up behind her. Alison flinched. 'I didn't intend to beat you up last night,' he continued. 'Bad case of nerves?'

'You could say that,' she answered glumly. 'I've already had a call from that other dragon, Deputy Chase.'

'I guess there's no way to put that man down,' Steady said, laughing. 'The word is out that the Springer smuggling ring is about to run a mission. The sheriff——'

'He's only a deputy. The sheriff is too smart to believe stupid things like that,' she interrupted.

'I see. Well, the deputy was interested in all our—I mean all the Task Force co-ordinating equipment. He wanted to make use of the facility.'

'And what did you tell him?' Alison was not a qualified Thespian. Her voice broke in the middle of the question, drawing a smile from Steady.

'What else could I say? Naturally we would want the facility to be available to *all* law enforcement officers.' Now it's *we* instead of *they*, Alison noted. His grin was broader as he searched her crestfallen face before he added, 'But, of course, he comes a day too late. Everything has been dismantled. I really hated to disappoint him.'

'Yes——' she gulped a deep breath '—I can see you would be—disappointed, that is.' Her knees were just the tiniest bit shaky. She felt behind her for the arm of one of the easy chairs and collapsed into it. 'Deputy Chase is really a nice man—but he's got this fixation.'

'And you haven't any idea why?'

'Not a bit,' she lied brazenly. He took the chair opposite her and leaned forward.

'That's not why I was hunting you, Alison.'

'No?' It was hard to keep the desperation out of her voice, but she tried. 'I can't imagine what *else* we have to discuss. Not after last night. I said goodbye, and I meant it, Mr Colson.'

'Don't you really know?'

She suddenly found the mosaic in the braided rug very interesting. Anything to avoid looking into those eyes. But only for a moment. Be bold, Mrs Santoso had said. That's the only way we will all escape from this trap. Brazen it out, all the way, Alison! She lifted her head and stared him straight in the eye.

'The last person who looked me straight in the eye like that was an axe-murderer who proceeded to tell me the biggest lie I ever heard,' he said pensively. 'You were going to say something?'

'Yes,' she snarled. 'You lawyers think you're so darn smart, don't you? Well, I want you to know that I have *never*—did you hear that?—*never* ever done anything like last night. Not in my whole life! And I don't care whether you believe it or not. I think I must have been out of my mind! Too much sun, or something like that.'

'And, do you know,' he said with a chuckle, 'I believe every word of it. Something you ate, perhaps! I've seen rabbits with more courage, Alison. Talk about the reluctant virgin!'

Perversely, the moment he made the remark she felt the crazy urge to declare him wrong. 'A lot you know,' she snarled. 'I've had plenty of experience. It was just *you* that turned me off!'

She got up from the chair and went to the window so she wouldn't have to guard her face so much. Carmen was just driving up in the minivan. Certainly there hadn't been enough time for a shopping trip. And the van careened down along the track towards the barn, rather than stopping in front of the house. Alison saw, but could not comprehend. Her mind was too full of the closeness of him, just behind her back.

'I really turn you off, do I?' His voice was right at her ear, low and seductive. His hands touched her shoulders and pulled her around.

'Yes,' she muttered wildly, feeling all her composure slip away. 'Absolutely.' The end of the word went up the scale and ended in a squeak of alarm as his left hand moved to the small of her back and pressed her hard up against him. Fight back, she screamed at herself. You don't want to end up a basket case at the mercy of your glands! Fight back!

His free hand circled her neck, and then began a slow progression downwards towards her vulnerable breasts. Only anger or pain could break her free, and she could not work up to anger. So instead, fearing the result worse than the act, she bit her own lower lip, tasted the blood, and *then* the anger came.

'Don't—do—this—to—me!' she screamed, accenting every word. 'Why should you hate me so much?' The grin on his face faded away. The pressure of his arms relaxed slightly, just enough for her to squirm away from him. She could still taste the blood on her lip, the anger in her heart.

Free, she moved a foot or two away, sobbing. No tears came, only the dry hacking sobs as she stood there defiantly, all five-foot four, her hair down in mad disarray, and her breast heaving from the dry cough.

'Oh, lord,' he muttered. 'Alison——'

Hearing her name served as the release valve. She turned and ran for the door.

'Alison!' he yelled at her. 'I love you!'

She stopped for a second at the door and railed at him. 'Sure you do, Steady. That's why you treat me so nicely!'

And then she was out of the door, on to the porch, down the stairs to the ground, letting the rain wash her face, her hair, her body, her soul.

But there was no escape from peril. Little Juanita was standing in front of her, so agitated that she kept shifting her weight from one foot to the other in an anxious sort of rain dance.

'Carmen dice, venga pronto,' the girl repeated for the third time. 'Come! Trouble. Plenty trouble!'

How could there *be* more trouble than this? Alison thought as she mastered her weak knees and followed the child down towards the barn.

'There *has* to be some mix-up,' Alison insisted. Pablo, sitting opposite her on a bale of hay, shrugged his shoulders. Carmen, more excited than Alison had ever seen her, maintained a stubborn silence.

'You met Pedro Santoso on the road into town? And that's exactly what he said?'

'Exactly,' Carmen said morosely. 'He say the Maldinado place is raided this morning. They take everything and everyone away. The sheriff's men, and that Miss Glebe. She comes to the raid, too.' Alison shook her head. It *could* get worse. Lord, it *had got* worse! The Maldinado place, on the south side of San Antonio, down at Poteet, was their organisation's only local back-up site. And the Maldinados themselves knew everything there was to be known about the operation!

Alison took a deep breath and swallowed hard. Now is the time for all good men, she repeated in her mind.

'Señor Santoso, he say time for us to run,' Carmen moaned. 'Crazy, that man. We *all* get arrested and thrown in *calabozo* for nine hundred years, no? Mr Santoso says, eh, what is more important? What can I say to question like that? They have everything ready in the *barrio*. But *they* don't have to drive the trip, no?'

'I'm afraid that Pedro is right,' Alison sighed. 'We have to move this shipment out. If we can get away with it, they won't be able to prove a thing—providing nobody talks. Pablo?'

The big Mayan stood up. He had been quiet all during the discourse, holding back. 'I don't know,' he said. 'Good or bad, I can't judge the ideas. But if you say go, Alison, I know that's the thing to do, and I go. Even if I have to go alone.'

Alison felt the stab in her heart. Through half a dozen years these two had become her best friends, her closest relatives, her greatest loves. And now *she* must make the choice, appoint the sacrifice. She stifled a tear with her knuckle. 'Go?' she said hesitantly.

Carmen shrugged her shoulders. 'I load the van. We can go—maybe earlier than usual?'

'You'd come with me?' Pablo's face lit up.

'Of course I come,' his wife said. 'I don't come, you get lost or something. Only I am scare, *linda.*'

'I—think Mr Santoso is right about what's important,' Alison said slowly. 'What can I say? We must try to do what we can. Pablo, do you need anything special?'

'No entiendo,' the big Guatemalman said. 'But you say go, I go.'

'Carmen?'

The little woman shrugged her shoulders. 'We knew all along it comes to this sometime,' she sighed. 'I am like Pablo. I don't understand either. But if you say go— we go.'

Oh, Gran, Alison thought. So we've come to the end of the road. And I forgot what you told me. Enjoy your yesterdays, because there may be no tomorrows. 'Then that's all there is to say,' she said quietly. 'We go. You have the maps and the names, Carmen?'

'Here. Only one map. Everything on tissue paper. And no Anglo guide.'

'But you can make the trip?'

'Seguro. We have been this way before. And you?'

'I'll stay and see if I can be conspicuous. If they watch the house and see me here, it might be a useful diversion.' Both Guatemalans nodded.

'Then, as soon as it gets dark, *amigos.* Get everything loaded and be ready for—say—ten o'clock. And Pablo— the sheriff's men are everywhere. If they stop you, no arguments. No fighting. Understand?'

The trio went back to the house, carrying the two children. Serious discussion stopped as the adults played with the babies. Even Pablo, for once, came down off his macho dignity and sprawled on the floor to entertain.

At four o'clock Alison got up off her knees, laughing. 'It's been fun,' she said, 'but I think I have to put in an appearance in the kitchen. Dinner won't make itself.'

Carmen struggled to her not-so-agile feet beside Alison. 'It will go well,' she encouraged. 'I have pray to *San Jaime*. You will see. Be brave.'

There was really very little to be done in the kitchen. The two women had laid on every preparation at various times during the day. Alison set the pork chops simmering on the stove, and all the vegetables were prepared in separate dishes for warming. She made doubly sure that everything was going well, and then headed for the bathroom.

It was unfair, she realised, to monopolise the only bathroom in the house so close to the dinner hour, but she felt the need. 'To prepare the sacrifice?' she muttered to herself as she undressed.

It was perhaps her worst fault. At least Gran had always chided her about her wry sense of humour. 'Gallows humour,' her grandmother had called it. And here she was, polishing up the body in case she was arrested. And clean new underwear. Another of Gran's strictures. 'Always wear new underwear when you go to the city. No telling when you might have an accident!'

Too many memories. As she slipped on her shower-cap and stepped into the warm water they came rushing back to her. Her beautiful, wan mother, lying on her big bed, trying to be cheerful, knowing she was close to death's door. Funny for a girl so young—that she would only remember her mother on that last day. Carefully she soaped and scrubbed.

A wild picture—Steady, crashing into the shower and trying to lift her out, with his hands slipping until they encompassed her breasts, at which point the balloon went up for both of them. Wasn't that a strange thing?

And when she tried to recall her father, she could not remember his face. Every time she thought of him it was Steady she saw. *That* thought startled her. 'All this time I thought it was love, and instead it's a father fixation,' she told herself.

That ended the reverie—and the shower. She turned off the water and climbed out, pursued by ghosts. Her cap had slipped, soaking a major portion of her long, heavy hair. She struggled with a towel, but more was needed. And she was being pressed. A knock on the bedroom door. 'Are you dead in there?' Steady Colson, back again!

'I'm sorry,' she yelled through the door. 'I thought you had left. I'll be out in just a minute.' Why in the name of heaven was he back? she thought. I'll have to get rid of him somehow. This is no night to have a lawman sitting in the house; not when so much is at stake! Without knowing exactly how to handle the situation, she threw on her robe over a still-wet body, gathered up her towels and clothing, and burst out of the bathroom in a cloud of steam, almost knocking him down.

'I *did* leave, but my mother told me I ought to come back,' he said facetiously. 'She said something about it not being neighbourly, leaving people alone in a storm like this. Can I stay for supper?' But she had gone down the hall before he could add the joke he had been perfecting about a weak kidney.

Dinner was a strange meal. Carmen had a great deal to say about the babies, but she said it all in Quiché, and even Alison couldn't catch the drift of the rapid-fire Indian dialect. Alison sat in her usual seat and feasted on misery.

'You don't like pork chops?' Steady asked when Carmen allowed him a respite in her conversation.

'I—like them fine,' she stammered. 'I—am just not hungry tonight——' She was about to add something else, but Carmen interrupted.

'We mus' get the children to bed now,' she said. 'They are up late last night, and work hard today, you know?' The little Guatemalan family sorted itself out. Alison hugged them all. It was difficult not to be too expressive. Steady Colson was a man who noted every nuance. After they had gone Alison found it hard to make conversation, and yet she dared not order him out. With Carmen and Pablo getting themselves moving, this was no time to send Steady Colson out of the house. He must be anchored, at least for a time. And so, to anchor him, she asked him about his mother, about Oklahoma, about California. Somehow, things went along. At last, looking over her shoulder out of the front window, she saw the minivan roll by the house, all its lights out. She slumped back into her chair, worn by deception, and stared glumly at him. Now she had a more delicate problem. If she didn't get away from him for a few minutes she was going to blow up in his face. And at the same time he must be kept where he was. The longer he stayed now, the further Carmen and Pablo could get down the road before pursuit could be organised.

'I have to go out and check something,' she said.

'Go out? On this kind of a night? That's silly.'

'I promised Carmen.' With all that time to spare, Alison had still not thought of an excuse. And ideas were not her strong suit at the moment, with her whole body shaking and her mind in a whirl. 'Juanita,' she said. 'I promised Carmen that I would come down and read Juanita a bedtime story.'

'That's great,' he said. 'I'll come along, too. And we don't have to go out in the rain. We can walk down the corridor!' Which was, of course, the last thing that Alison wanted to have happen.

'No.' Almost a shout, that, and then she came to her senses. 'This is supposed to be strictly girl-talk. And I have to use the outside door so I won't disturb Pablo and Carmen. You can't come!' And then, much less firmly, 'And I'm going.'

'Some crazy logic,' Steady called after her. 'I thought we might have a talk tonight.'

'Perhaps,' she offered vaguely as she grabbed her raincoat and headed outside. It took fifteen minutes of plodding up and down, getting herself thoroughly soaked, before she regained control of herself. The most dangerous wolf in the world was the beast in hiding. Steady Colson was that wolf. But as long as he was here, incommunicado, the less that danger would be. He could not have seen the minivan leave. He had been looking in the wrong direction. And as long as she could keep him entertained, just that much longer would Pablo and Carmen have to go north and make contact! And how, her conscience asked, do you keep him incommunicado, little Miss Alison? Strangle him? Tie him up? Seduce him?

Alison shuddered as she turned around and resolutely made for the front door again.

'You really are wet,' he said as she came in. 'Don't tell me Juanita is sleeping outside?' He ignored the glare she awarded him.

'No? Am I wet?' she asked. Come on, Alison, she told herself. This isn't the way to vamp him! Or tie him up, either. She stopped in front of the wall-mirror in the hall. 'Why, I really am,' she announced, as if it had all surprised her. Here I am on the attack, she thought. Have you ever seen a more poorly armed attacker? 'I'd better dry off and change. You can stay a while?'

'All the while you want,' he said expansively. 'I don't think my mother is waiting up for me. Maybe I'll call and assure her.'

'That's not possible,' she said hurriedly. 'The telephone's been out of order for a while. The storm and the rains, you know.'

'I'm not really worried about my mother,' he said, laughing. 'I'm a big boy. She'll expect me when she sees me, and not before. You'd better scoot before you catch influenza.'

'Yes,' she stammered. 'I'd—better do that. You wait here—please?'

She didn't dare to spend the time a shower would take. He might get footloose, and wander—and find that the house was empty! So instead she rubbed herself down with a big bath-towel, hastily found a pair of trousers and a blouse, bundled her hair up, and headed for the kitchen. A pot of hot chocolate did not require a great deal of effort. Which was fortunate, if you were a girl whose hands were trembling, whose mind was rebelling, whose body was not sure what orders to follow.

But when she came back into the living-room he was still sitting there, reading an old magazine. 'You do look different,' he acknowledged. 'Hot chocolate! I haven't had that in years!' He patted the couch beside him, but she quickly manoeuvred herself into the armchair opposite.

'I thought we might—play chess.'

The big smile on his face faded. 'Chess?'

'You do play, don't you? All lawyers play chess.'

'Oh, I play all right,' he said. 'Why, it was only—twenty-five years ago that I had my last match! I *do* know a couple of other parlour games I'd prefer.'

'I only play chess,' she announced with considerable firmness.

'So chess,' he sighed. 'Even my mother wouldn't believe this, Alison!' She decided to ignore the comment, and went to fetch the board. He needed help in setting up the pieces. 'Maybe it was twenty-seven years ago,' he commented.

The first game lasted three minutes, and ended in a fool's mate. Alison felt better immediately. At least there was *something* he wasn't perfect at. The second went for thirty minutes, and ended in total disaster as she lost her queen through stupidity. But in the third game age and maturity told. Her age and his maturity. Somewhere around eleven o'clock Alison decided to rest her eyes for just a second before she made her next move and fell instantly asleep; it was three in the morning when the flashing red lights and the siren on the police cruiser, which had pulled up outside the house, woke her.

A fist hammered on the door. Nothing polite, nothing fancy, just your old-fashioned police pounding. By the time Alison got to the door, Steady was half-awake, grumbling. When she opened the door Deputy Sheriff Chase forced his way by her and stood in the middle of the room, threatening. By this time Steady, his sandy hair all in bushy disarray, waited and watched with an inscrutable face.

'Well, we've got you this time,' the deputy announced.

'Have you?' She was so sleepy that her mind was not yet in gear. 'Got me for what?'

'Got you for smuggling. I have to read you your rights, Alison Springer,' the burly man said as he whipped out a little card and proceeded to do just that. She collapsed back into Carmen's rocker as Steady came up behind her and put a supportive hand on her shoulder.

'You don't have to answer any questions,' Colson advised her.

'I don't mind answering any questions *he* can think of,' she replied gently. 'What have you caught me at, Deputy?'

'We caught your Mexican pair on the road with that minivan of yours,' he said, almost licking his chops with satisfaction. 'My men are down the road searching it now. You might as well confess, Miss Alison.'

'They're not Mexican,' she said firmly. 'They're American citizens of Guatemalan descent. Is it illegal for a husband and wife to go off in my minivan?'

'All the way to Austin in the rain?' He chuckled. 'You can't fool me, Miss Alison. I been around in this business too long.'

'Yes, I can see that, Deputy.' Alison stretched out both hands in his direction. They were no longer trembling, she noted, pleased with herself. When push came to shove, Alison Springer was prepared for battle. 'I suppose this is where you put the cuffs on me? Or is there a third degree before that?'

'That'll come,' he promised. 'Judge Hacket is waiting at his home for us to come by. By tomorrow dawn you'll be in the county jail, young lady. Unless you'd care to tell us all about it now? I know there are others behind you. Give us the names, and maybe—just *maybe*—things might go easier with you!'

'Alison, you don't have to answer anything,' Steady repeated. 'Do you want me to be your lawyer?'

'Wouldn't that look good in the morning paper?' she asked him. 'Justice Department Official Represents Small-Time Smuggler?'

'I'm not a justice department official,' Steady said with a trace of impatience.

'Aha, you admit you're a smuggler.' The deputy chortled.

'No, I don't admit anything.' She rocked back and forth a couple of times, watching the sheriff's officer. 'You really mean I could get off easier if I name the higher-ups——?'

'Don't say another word,' Steady interrupted. She flashed him a weak smile. He took her hand.

'You surely can, Miss Alison.' The big deputy was all kindness as he whipped a notebook out of his pocket. 'You go ahead, little lady.'

'Well,' she said, licking her lips as she started. 'First there's Mayor Rodriques, of San Antonio. He's the local man. Then there's Governor Childress, up in the state capital, and then—there's the President of the United States. They're all directly involved. Oh, did I forget the Attorney General? And all the Senators and Congressmen? They're all my accomplices.'

'Damn!' the deputy swore as he snapped his notebook shut. 'With that kind of talk, girl, I'm gonna lock you up and throw away the key!' His face flushed. 'Where the hell are those people?' he exclaimed.

As if on cue, another police cruiser, its red light flashing, came around the bend in the road, followed by the little old minivan. The little cavalcade came to a stop at the front door, and two more deputies came into the house, leaving their motor running and their lights still flashing.

'Well?' Deputy Chase demanded.

The first man shrugged his shoulders. The second looked everywhere but at the deputy. 'Nothing,' he said. 'Not a damn thing!'

'In that case we'll take them over to the sheriff's office and really pull that car apart,' Chase snarled.

'Now just a darn minute.' Alison got up from her chair. She was visibly trembling now, shaking so hard that Steady stalked across the room, forced the sheriff to step aside, and put an arm around her shoulders. She managed a weak smile, and ducked her head for a moment into the warmth of his shoulder, forgetting who her real enemy was.

'You arrested my employees south of Austin, did you?' she asked.

'Yeah,' Chase said. 'So what?'

'And you think you're going to get away with taking them—and those little kids—down to the lock-up?'

'Well—I——'

'Yeah,' the second deputy said. 'Two little kids, fast asleep.'

Steady moved into command, touching Alison's lips with a cautionary finger. 'You have the parents and two little children out there in the rain, Deputy?' he asked gently. 'Isn't there an election coming up in October? I believe I heard that the Hispanic vote has outgrown every other ethnic group in the county. You could be unemployed, Deputy. Think what that would mean to your wife and kids.'

'Don't threaten me!' the deputy roared. 'They're using those kids as a cover-up.'

'Then don't threaten these people,' Steady returned. His tone was no longer gentle. 'Get those kids in out of the rain. Now!'

The deputy jumped as if someone had attacked him with a cattle-prod. 'Get them in here, Jim!' he snarled. A moment later Carmen and Pablo came in, each of them carrying one of the sleeping girls. Carmen went straight to the rocking-chair, and plumped herself into it, exhausted.

'Oh, I am scared,' she said. 'These—they stop us on the road for no reason, and shout and scream and wake up the babies, and make all kinds of threats. Why they do this?'

CHAPTER NINE

THE baby whimpered as Carmen sat down in the chair. Carmen patted her back gently in a circular motion until she slept again. Juanita, draped over Pablo's shoulder, opened one eye, found nothing of interest, and she, too, went back to sleep. With Carmen seated, they traded children.

'Now, let me get this straight,' Steady said. 'You were driving down the road going about your lawful business, when this crowd stopped you. You weren't speeding or anything like that?'

'That's one old van,' Pablo said. 'Can't get more than fifty miles an hour out of it; no matter how you try. Nope, they stopped us for no reason at all.'

'What do you know?' Steady mused. 'Search and seizure without a warrant. You don't have a warrant, Deputy?'

I should bake a cake for this frosting he's spreading, Alison thought, and had to suppress a giggle. Lord, I'm scared of him, and he's not even talking to me!

'Well, I don't exactly have one here,' Chase muttered. 'I didn't need one. We was in hot pursuit. Law says we can act in pursuit of a criminal.'

'That's the trouble with law,' Steady continued in that same smooth voice. 'Too many people read sentences and think they understand chapters! Or am I mistaken, Mr Chase? What school did you get your law degree from?'

There was the sound of another car driving up outside. The officer, listening, smiled and regained some of his courage. 'I don't need a law degree,' he said. 'Not when my lawyer just drove up. You just wait one minute, buster, and we'll see who's who.'

It took longer than a minute. The front door banged open and Harriet Glebe came in. Even in the early hours of the morning she was dressed in her usual sophistication. For a second Alison felt despair again. There was just no way a country girl could compete with this— woman. But, on the other hand, what was she competing for? Steady? She had already abandoned all hope in his direction. But the more he talked here tonight— she couldn't have *everything* so mixed up, could she?

A grand entrance required preparation, beauty, and an audience. Harriet posed in the doorway, and found she had attracted something more than the gathering she wanted. Weary old Michael, the sheepdog who spent most of his life asleep on the rug in the corner, opened one eye, and evidently didn't like what he saw. He worked up one tremendous growl, which did not have the effect he wanted. Clumsily, he worked his way up to his feet, growled again, and walked stiff-legged over to the door to confront the woman.

'Get that animal away from me,' Harriet said, half in anger, half in fear. Michael smelled the fear and tried another growl. 'Get him away from me!'

'He wouldn't hurt a fly,' Alison cautioned as she moved slowly up behind Michael. As with any animal, she knew that a sudden noise would startle the dog and send him into some sort of action, good or bad. 'Nice Michael. Down boy.'

The dog ignored her, taking a couple of steps forward and showing his teeth. Now a Texas sheep-dog, a border collie, was not the biggest dog in the world. But even so, they all possessed a mean-looking set of teeth, and tended to keep them into old age. So, although Michael might not have the strength to out-wrestle a jack rabbit, or the speed to catch a three-toed sloth, to any stranger he still looked exceedingly dangerous. Especially when his mouth was open and he was growling. Harriet Glebe was a woman who operated on the very edge of panic. Michael's appearance was just enough to send her over the precipice. She screamed once, a high-pitched, piercing shriek that tore at Michael's sensitive ears. The dog whined and moved forward a pace or two. Feeling threatened, Harriet swung her shoulder bag at Michael's head, and simultaneously kicked out at him with her foot.

The foot landed, jarring the dog sidewise. Michael was a great believer in the thesis that he who runs away need not fight until another day. The kick convinced him it was time to run, but his hindquarters were slipping on the wood floor, his head was aimed in the wrong direction, and all he managed to do was to bang into Harriet Glebe just about at knee level, with all the force he could muster. The pair of them sprawled on top of each other. It was hard to tell which one was the most frightened, and which one was doing the most scrambling to get away.

'All right, now.' Alison moved into the affray, catching Michael by his collar and pulling him away from the woman. The dog was eager to be convinced. He skidded around behind his mistress's protective shape, uttered one more bark of bravado and sat down, waiting for approval.

Steady came over to help Harriet to her feet. The woman was gibbering. She clung to Colson with both arms, shaking. He was doing his best to comfort the hysterical woman, and, eventually, his best was good enough. 'Stedman,' she said. 'Thank heaven you're here.

Did you see that? She set her dog on me. You'll be my witness. Deputy Chase, shoot that animal!'

Deputy Clarence Chase was a Texas 'ole boy', a member in good standing of the Elks, the Moose, the Democratic Party, and the American Legion. He might not have been the brightest man in the world. After all, when God made the average man, he made a very great many below-average men to balance the scales! Tell Chase to arrest his brother and he would; but tell him to shoot a sheepdog—now, that was another question indeed. 'Not me, Ms Glebe,' he drawled. 'He ain't done nothin' no normal dog wouldn't do. You scared him.'

'I demand that you shoot that dog!' Harriet yelled. The deputy stubbornly shook his head.

'Then give me your damn gun and I'll do it for myself,' she screamed, trying to snatch the officer's weapon from its holster. But Alison, who had played a spectator role up to that moment, had her hand in first. 'Nobody hurts my dog,' she said in a stilted angry tone. *'Nobody.'*

But Harriet Glebe was out for vengeance now. Not for the dog's minor foray, but for all the real and imagined wrongs she had experienced at the hands of the Springer family. 'Stedman,' she said with a hollow voice, 'she's holding a gun on me! I'm going to bring her up on so many charges she won't see the sun again for the rest of her life. Take it away from her!'

Stedman Colson took a step or two away from Harriet and towards Alison. Allie handed him the gun and then dropped to her knees to comfort Michael. 'Stedman,' Harriet demanded, holding out her hand for the gun. He grinned at her, a tight-lipped grin that spoke volumes. 'Stedman?'

'There's a difference between prosecution and per-secution,' Steady Colson said. 'If you intend to bring

Alison up on charges—on any charges—I'll defend her. If she'll have me. Alison?'

'Yes. Yes, of course,' she said. Her head was on a roller-coaster ride, seated just behind her heart. The world was a puzzling place. Thunder sounded while birds sang, and she could see the rain through the front window. 'Have I made another mistake?' she queried softly.

'Not really,' he murmured, helping her to her feet. 'Not really.' He put one arm around her. She leaned against it, needing the support. It had been altogether one heck of a day, and it wasn't over yet!

Steady passed the gun back to Deputy Chase, who holstered it without a word. 'Now, then,' Colson said, 'where were we? Oh, yes, you stopped and seized this pair of fine American citizens without a warrant. I hope you had a very good reason, Deputy. If not, I'm going to sue each one of you—and your lawyer—for false arrest. Alison, paper and pencil, please. Write down the names of all these—people—so we don't miss any of them in our suit!'

'Hey, now!' Chase blustered. 'You can't do that.'

'I can't?' The mask was off. Steady Colson was a shark, circling, looking for a place to bite. His soft voice had hardened.

'I—well——' the Deputy stuttered. 'We—don't need these people, but I'm going to take that car down to the police garage and search it from end to end.'

'Oh, Stedman,' Harriet wailed. 'It's a good, solid case. Why do you have to get into it now? These people—they mean nothing to us.'

'Ah, but they do,' he replied. 'Each and every one of them mean a great deal to me.'

'As much as I do?'

He looked up and down as if he were seeing her for the first time. 'More than you do,' he said. 'I don't think I'd be very happy married to a law-book. I want a woman who is all woman. Somebody who can laugh and love and share, not quote a precedent. Now, Alison—about the van?'

'I—it's all right if they take it,' she whispered, hardly able to muster a voice. She had heard so much! She had been so wrong! And in a little while he would be bound to find out the secret behind it, the secret that would send him away from her again! She nibbled at her lip until she drew blood. 'The car's all right,' she repeated.

'Hear that?' Steady asked the deputy. 'The lady feels like being kind to you. I don't agree, but she's my client, and that makes her the boss, you understand.' The silky-soft voice was back, with a hint of steel behind the words. 'For a minute there I was just about to show you I *could* stop you, but since the lady of the house feels you should get away with it, then I won't push—tonight, that is. Tomorrow I might just wander down to the office and have a few more words with you. And now I think we can excuse you—Deputy.'

Chase turned several shades of red and purple and stomped out of the house, his assistants trailing him nervously. Harriet Glebe, almost in tears, took a step or two towards the door, then turned. 'Stedman,' she said, 'think of all the things we could be together. The best families, the best law firm, the jet set, money. Maybe——' A frog caught in her throat and she coughed before continuing. 'Maybe even a child, if you want it so badly.'

Steady stared at her, but kept his arm around Alison's shoulders. 'Goodbye, Miss Glebe,' he said coldly. Harriet sobbed and ran for the door, slamming it behind her. Outside, car engines roared, wheels spun, and sirens sounded again as the law-men disappeared into the rain. There was a light on the horizon. It was almost dawn.

Inside the house, deadly silence filled the room. Alison did her best to become invisible. Carmen sat and rocked Juanita, while Pablo moved over to the couch and gently lay Conchita down on it. The baby stirred and whimpered.

'Now that we're rid of the police,' Colson said, 'I think it's time one of you told me just what's going on here.' There followed an even deeper silence, broken only by a colicky little cry from Conchita.

Carmen rocked back and forth at a faster cadence. 'Why we make all the noises?' she complained. 'Wake up the babies. And those policemen. Bah! Next time I don't vote Anglo!'

Her husband said a few words to her in Spanish, but instead of quieting her it had the opposite effect. 'Why I be quiet?' she raged. 'I don't do nothin'!'

'No, you didn't do anything,' Steady said. 'All you did was go off in the rain, taking your babies for a ride. What a perfect cover *that* is for smuggling. Who could doubt or disturb a pair of sleeping kids?'

'Is a law to say not take babies for a ride?' Carmen replied grimly. 'They sleep good on auto ride. Go five miles, they all asleep!'

'Excellent,' Steady said. 'You'll make a great witness. Now it's your turn, Alison.' She ducked her head. Little Conchita began to whimper. 'I don't have anything to say,' Alison replied. 'I have Constitutional rights.'

'You bet,' he said, sounding like some friendly uncle. 'But you don't quite know what they are.'

'I'll hire a lawyer,' she replied grumpily. 'There are so many lawyers in San Antonio, you can rent them by the dozen—in any language, too.'

'Come on, Alison Springer,' he coaxed. 'It's your turn. Now is the time for all good Alisons to tell the truth, the whole truth, and——' Conchita, disappointed in the lack of attention, tried out one full-throated wail, and then began to cry in earnest. 'Well, isn't anybody going to help the poor little tyke?'

Nobody moved. 'No? Then I'll do it myself!'

'No!' Alison almost ran to get in front of him. 'No, you can't help. She's a little baby, and you don't have any experience with babies, and——'

Steady looked down at her, a shrewd look playing across his angled face. 'Now what in the world can you all be hiding?' he mused. 'And I had plenty of experience. When I was way back there in Middle School I used to hire out as a baby-sitter. You have no idea how many nappies I've changed in my time. And although that's lots of years ago, I don't think they've made any changes in the basic model, have they?'

'No,' Alison admitted, almost breathlessly. 'But I'll take care of the baby.'

'No, now that I think of it,' Steady said, 'I think I'll do it myself. I figure to get married one of these days soon, and, who knows, the extra training may come in handy.' With a hand on each of Alison's elbows, he lifted her clear off her feet and set her to one side. Carmen and Alison stared at each other. Pablo shrugged his shoulders. Steady turned to the baby.

'Hey, now, little bit,' he crooned as he reached for her nappy pins. 'Wet pants, have we? Not to worry. Uncle Steady will fix it all up high and dry.' He tickled the baby, rubbing a gentle finger across her navel. Conchita kicked her feet and smiled at him through half-closed eyes. 'And now,' he said, 'we take out this other pin, and—any extra nappies, Carmen?'

'In the bag,' the Guatemalan said. She gave him a wintry smile and looked back at Alison. Steady leaned over to pick up the travel-bag. 'Ah, disposables,' he said as he pulled one out of the package. 'I haven't worked with that sort of thing before. Now, then, little lovely.' The second pin came open as he spread the nappy out and pulled down the old. 'And then, as easy as peaches in cream, we—what the hell?'

He was a man of some experience, no doubt about that. He held one broad-spread hand on the baby's stomach while he looked around the room. Three pairs of adult eyes did their best to avoid his. Carmen said something softly in Quiché to her husband. *'Fatalidad,'* Pablo responded. 'Fate.' The pair of them shrugged and turned to watch.

'You don't watch out,' pragmatic Carmen added in her best English, 'and he gonna squirt you.'

'Alison!' Steady prodded angrily. 'Just what the hell have you been smuggling?'

She squared around to face him, pushing her shoulders back, holding her head high. 'What else?' she sighed. 'Babies!'

The inquisition began the next day, shortly after noon, in the living-room of the ranch-house. Carmen, busy in the corner rocking-chair, with a bowl full of green beans to be snapped; Abigail Colson, unable to stifle her yawns, cuddling the little boy in her arms as she watched her stiffly controlled son pace up and down. And Alison, determined to brave out everything, fingering her neck as if expecting the headsman's axe.

'Now,' Steady said, enunciating each word sharply as if words were to replace gavel-thumping in the court of last resort, 'I think we need to examine the whole problem. Smuggling babies. What a crazy idea.'

'It's not crazy at all,' Alison said firmly, but when he turned to look in her direction she ducked her head out of the line of fire.

'Well, don't leave it lying there,' he said sarcastically.

'You talk like that because you're ignorant,' she charged. 'All these babies are orphans. Their parents have been killed in the crazy revolutions going on in Central America. If nobody brought them out—the babies would be dead, too! Somebody had to do something about it. But the Federals won't help, and the State people won't have anything to do with them. Babies? Lord, who wants a thousand Indian babies? They can't vote!'

'If we are going to arrive at some solution,' he cautioned, 'we have to do it logically, not emotionally.'

'A lot you know,' she scoffed. 'Gran tried logic for years, and never rescued a single child. Not one—until we turned emotional.'

'Oh, come on! Gran organised this scam?'

'Well, really Alison does it. But Gran, she help,' Carmen interrupted. 'Six years, we run. One thousand sixty-two babies we rescue. Including these two, no? You ever done such much good, Mr Colson?'

'I don't think so,' he drawled. 'And never once got caught?'

'Of course not,' the Guatemalan woman snorted. 'Why? Because they send *men* to catch us. They look, they don't even see what under the nose is! Like last night.'

'Now just let me back up here a bit,' he sighed. 'The first day I came here there were two little girls. I'm sure of that. Now suddenly Conchita turns out to be a boy. What happened?'

'Our staff work sometimes gives us trouble,' Alison explained. 'We have birth certificates for two little girls.

When a boy shows up, he has to be disguised. They always use the names Juanita and Conchita, because that's what the certificates say. Although actually Conchita was named Juan, you know. We shipped that other pair north on the day you first came, and these two little darlings arrived the next day. We have to keep to a schedule. Otherwise kids will be backed up all along the network, and then the fat would really be in the fire. Only we hadn't been told that Conchita had a leg-wound. That caught us by surprise, and almost gave the game away.'

'And this pair, they'll go soon?'

'Soon,' Alison replied. 'And that's when it really hurts. We keep them down here long enough to check on health, inoculations, that sort of thing. It's not very long, but long enough so that it breaks our hearts when they have to go. But—there are so many more that need to come, we have to push them on. It got so bad that we had to start referring to them as "packages" instead of people.'

'When, exactly?' he asked. 'When do this pair have to go?'

Alison, her hands balled up into fists, glared at him. 'I'm not going to tell you about the rest of the network!'

'All right,' he agreed, 'I'll leave that for the moment. But, Carmen, when you went north yesterday you *must* have had a list of contacts, a map, that sort of thing. And yet the police found nothing?'

'They didn't find the map, or the name of the next contact?' Alison asked anxiously.

'Like I say, nothing.' Carmen giggled. 'They stop the truck, no? They even bring woman officer to search *me*. All my clothes off I must take. And Pablo the same. But they don't find the map, they don't find the list, nothing.'

'I'm not sure I want to know, but how did they miss?' Steady asked.

'Easy. I put the papers in the baby's nappy. Whoever gonna search inside a dirty nappy? You want spinach with supper also, Alison?'

'Whoa, don't change the subject. So you've been smuggling babies into the United States for years, from——'

'From Guatemala,' Alison filled in. 'They are not all natives of Guatemala. It's just that we have a sort of gathering centre there, a shipping terminal. And we *don't* smuggle them *into* the United States.'

'So let's not quibble,' he sighed. 'You're breaking the law six ways from Sunday.'

'I'm not quibbling,' Alison said doggedly. 'We're smuggling babies *through* the United States, not *into* it. Our Underground Railroad has eight stops, the last one in Toronto. The Canadians aren't as darn stiff-necked and arrogant as the American Government.'

'Oh, lord.' Very suddenly, Colson looked as if his back hurt him. Or his head. 'Two border crossings?'

'Easiest part,' Carmen said gently. 'Crossing the border very simple. Setting up safe houses like this— very difficult. Especially when some crazy lawyer move into the middle of the operation. We all *little* people, you know—nobody important anywhere in our organisation.'

'There must be *someone* at the top,' he insisted.

'Gran was the chief,' Alison said quietly.

'And since she died?'

'She made me promise that I would stay and keep the network going for seven years. Gran believed in the biblical story of the seven lean years.'

'And that's why you've stayed in this rundown spread,' he said softly. 'You promised Gran!'

'Yes,' she flared. 'Some of us *have* to keep our promises.'

He shook his head sadly. 'You're a bag of surprises, Alison Springer. Here you are sitting in the middle of the biggest smuggling sweep in years, and I swear there's no way in the world they can stop you! Am I going to end up with pie in my face when *this* story comes out!'

'Do you—you don't think we'll all go to jail?' Alison stammered. 'Every time they tell me about that Huntsville Prison, I get the shakes something terrible.'

'Under ordinary circumstances, probably,' he agreed nonchalantly. 'A lot depends on the skill of the defence lawyer. Ten years for the ring leaders, I suppose, and four or five for the others. State jail, too. Chase was right, wasn't he, when he predicted they'd have to send you away to Huntsville? That's one *bad* place.'

'We don't go to jail before suppertime,' Carmen said in her practical no-nonsense voice. 'I finish the beans, Alison. Now I go take Pablo's place. He a good man, that one. Loves *all* the children; hates to see any of them go. People look on outside, they say, hah, big, dumb shepherd. I look on inside, see big, soft-hearted, loving man! Everybody should look *inside* people.' And with that enigmatic advice she got up and headed down the corridor to the east wing of the house.

'So now I suppose you're going to tell the sheriff?' Alison looked up at him, fighting back the tears. These were no longer casual words. 'Jail' and 'Huntsville' had come very close; so close that she could smell the walls, hear the crowded prisoners complaining.

'Well,' he drawled. 'I *am* an officer of the court. I *should* tell it all. On the other hand, I don't want to be made to look like a fool any more than you would. But if I don't tell them, and they subpoena me into court, then I'd have to tell the truth on the witness-stand, anyway, wouldn't I?'

'Yes, of course.' Alison had a headache. Now she could feel a stomach-ache coming on. Her shoulders slumped. What had been a little trickle of despair became a whole wagonload, all dumping on her head.

'Unless——' he said quietly.

Her head came up with a snap as he stopped pacing directly in front of her.

'Unless?' she questioned hopefully.

'There's one legal situation that would prevent them from even calling me to the stand,' he said. 'Would prevent them even from questioning me!'

'You mean you'd take the Fifth Amendment?' she asked.

'No. I mean I'd marry the star defendant,' he announced, with that curious twist of words that magicians use when they are about to pull rabbits out of a hat. 'A husband cannot be required to give evidence against his wife.'

'Marry?' Abigail interjected. 'What lovely words. I suppose they're not *just* words?'

'Look at it this way,' he told his mother. 'If I marry Alison, I keep her from going to jail, and that keeps Pablo and Carmen out, also. I keep from being made to look like a fool. I keep those babies who have passed through the chain out of trouble. And besides, Alison is a nice person. I love her. What say, Mother?'

'I think it's probably just the thing to do,' Abigail said. 'But it isn't me you have to convince. Why don't you take it up with the party of the first part?'

'Alison,' he called. 'Alison?' But it was no use. Just after that bit about 'Marry the star defendant', Alison Springer had gone off into outer space and had missed all the rest of the conversation. He leaned over and shook her arm.

'And that, I believe, is you,' he said, when her eyes came back in focus.

She stood up, trembling. Not this way, she screamed to herself. Not like some barter arrangement, so many debits on one side, and credits on the other! 'Harriet Glebe will be very unhappy,' she said crossly.

'No more than I if this all comes out in the papers,' he returned. She scanned his phlegmatic face, looking for some hint of trust, of love, of future. Somewhere, among all the words, spoken and unspoken, she knew she had missed something. A phrase, a look, a sentence—it had gone completely over her head and she was too upset, too tired, to look back and find it!

'Don't you think *I* would be unhappy, too?' she asked. He blinked rapidly a couple of times, but his expression did not change.

'Not as unhappy as if they sent you away to Huntsville.' He lowered his voice to that hypnotic baritone that so helped to daze her, but this time she was determined to fight back.

'And that's all you see of this marriage? A chance to save face? That's all you want from it?'

'If that's all *you* want of it, it will have to do, won't it?' he returned bleakly. 'I've told you everything on my side. Now what about you?'

'Then I warn you now, that's all you're going to get out of it!' she snapped. 'I'll rescue your pride and you'll keep me out of prison—and that's the whole of our relationship!'

'Better that than nothing. So be it,' he murmured, giving her a speculative look.

'And I don't intend to stop working with the smuggling network,' she threatened. 'I still owe Gran a little more on my promise!'

He smiled at her, a gentle, searching smile, and hugged her enthusiastically. She was so tired that she actually relaxed, and leaned against his chest. 'Well, in that case, you'd better fix me a packed lunch for my roadside meal,' he said.

'I—don't understand. Are you going someplace?'

'Of course I am.' He laughed. 'Can you get me that map and the names of the the people at the Central Texas drop-off point? The deputy and his men are going to be all day searching that minivan of yours, so this would be a perfect afternoon for a drive. And I know two little kids who ought to get up to Dallas this afternoon!'

Alison ducked her head between her hands, trying to stop the ringing echo in her ears. Nothing seemed right. Nothing. But she had to go on; there could be no turning back.

'They can't go in the daylight,' she said. 'We're the ones with experience. You may be a great trial lawyer, but we're the experienced smugglers. Tonight, late.' And there I've blown it, she thought, too late to recall the words. Not only he knows, but his mother knows, too! Good lord, what a fool I am! 'And now I need a nap,' she continued wearily. 'We've been up all night. We *all* need a nap.'

'Good idea,' he commented. 'I'm bushed myself. I'll nap here in Gran's room, if you don't mind?'

'I don't mind, but what about your mother?'

'I have a name,' Abigail teased them. 'And I'll put my feet up and dream about grandchildren. A half-dozen, at least.'

'Please, Mother,' Steady protested. 'Things are at a very delicate point.' But Alison was out of the room before the discussion went any further.

Her bedroom had become a sanctuary again. She pulled down the shades, hesitated a moment, then slipped into her nightgown. The sheets were cool and welcoming. Her eyelids were heavy; they fell of their own volition. Sleep was intermittent, as she wrestled with her problems. There were too many 'he said' and 'she said' statements to be remembered. But she did try, sleeping uneasily, coming awake with a start, sleeping again. Some time late in the afternoon, with only four hours' sleep behind her, she came awake with a shock, and sat up straight in her bed! He said! Could he possibly have said that?

Her fuzzy mind could not decide whether he had said it or not. But a determined woman like Alison Springer could leave nothing to chance. 'I'll go ask him,' she muttered.

Out of bed she bounced, neglecting robe and slippers. Out into the corridor, not noticing how sheer her nightgown really was. Down the corridor, bare feet slapping on the polished wood, and into Gran's room.

He wasn't asleep. Both curtains were up, and he was sitting with his back against a pile of pillows. As she came in he put down the book he was reading. 'What took you so long?' he asked. That big grin was back.

'I—couldn't remember,' she said cautiously. 'Move over.' He complied. It took a moment to settle herself down. Her mind, that was, not her body. And then she was ready.

'Tell me again what you said,' she demanded. Her head was on his shoulder. His arm came around behind her, hand resting just under the curve of her breast. She shivered.

'Everything I said?' he asked. 'That could take forever!'

'I've got that much time,' she murmured. 'Tell me what you said to your mother, after you listed all the nice reasons for our getting married!'

'Oh, that?'

She squirmed around to face him, crushing her breast against his arm. 'No, not "oh that",' she said. 'That other. You said we should get married because then I wouldn't have to go to jail and then you said——'

'I love you,' he replied solemnly.

'That's it! That's it,' she repeated excitedly. 'I—wasn't listening, and I didn't—and I do!'

'This is going to be some marriage,' he sighed. 'You do what?'

She wiggled some more, and managed to kiss the tip of his chin. 'I do anything you want to do,' she whispered. And then, aloud, 'Do you remember once you said I had a heart as big as Texas?'

'I remember,' he replied. 'I meant to ask you if there was room in there for me, but circumstances overwhelmed me.'

'Well, if you'll keep it a secret,' she said, 'I love you very much, Stedman Colson. There's room enough in my heart for you, for your mother, and for all those grandchildren she wants. What do you say to that?'

'We'll get married tomorrow,' he said. 'And, in the meantime, come over here.'

'Steady!' she squealed. 'It's afternoon, and all the shades are up!'

'That's what I like,' he laughed. 'A girl who knows everything, and hasn't anything else to say.'

She didn't. It's hard to talk when his lips have sealed your mouth, and his hands are doing marvellously indecent things!

Harlequin Presents

Coming Next Month

#1287 BELONGING Sally Cook
Mandy always knew she was adopted, but having grown up so different from her adoptive parents, she decides to trace her real mother. While her search is successful, she finds the attractive Grant Livingstone is highly suspicious of her motives.

#1288 THE ULTIMATE CHOICE Emma Darcy
According to Kelly, the new owner of Marian Park is an arrogant swine who betrayed her grandfather and who wants to ruin Kelly's show-jumping career Determined not to be stopped, she confronts Justin St. John, with all guns blazing....

#1289 TAKING CHANCES Vanessa Grant
It seems an odd request even for Misty's detective agency. Why does Zeb Turner want her to kidnap him? Finding out, Misty lands herself with more than she'd bargained for—maybe even more than she can cope with!.

#1290 RUNAWAY WIFE Charlotte Lamb
Francesca has everything, so it seems—Oliver, her handsome, successful husband; a healthy son; and a lovely home. She believes she's merely a symbol of his success to Oliver and needs—and wants—far more than that from life.

#1291 THE SEDUCTION OF SARA Joanna Mansell
Sara isn't too pleased to have Lucas Farraday following her around Peru. She thinks he's just a penniless drifter. Gradually she relaxes and gets used to his presence and his help. And that's when Lucas makes his next move..

#1292 RECKLESS HEART Kate Proctor
Ever since Sian McAllister's new boss, Nicholas Sinclair, had jumped to the wrong conclusions about her, life has been difficult. And the situation becomes impossible when Sian realizes that despite their strong disagreements, she's falling in love with him.

#1293 GENTLE DECEPTION Frances Roding
Rosy's love for her married cousin, Elliott, is entirely platonic, but not everyone sees it that way. To prove them wrong, Rosy has to find herself a man. Callum Blake is perfectly willing to be her pretend lover—yet what if pretence becomes reality?

#1294 DESIGNED WITH LOVE Kathryn Ross
Drew Sheldon is Amanda's ex-fiancé—and when her father sells the family firm to him, Amanda has a problem. She needs her job, but can she live with the power Drew now holds over her when she has an idea he really might want revenge?

Available in August wherever paperback books are sold, or through Harlequin Reader Service:

In the U.S.
901 Fuhrmann Blvd.
P.O. Box 1397
Buffalo, N.Y. 14240-1397

In Canada
P.O. Box 603
Fort Erie, Ontario
L2A 5X3

H A R L E Q U I N
American Romance

THE LOVES OF A CENTURY...

Join American Romance in a nostalgic look back at the Twentieth Century—at the lives and loves of American men and women from the turn-of-the-century to the dawn of the year 2000.

Journey through the decades from the dance halls of the 1900s to the discos of the seventies ... from Glenn Miller to the Beatles ... from Valentino to Newman ... from corset to miniskirt ... from beau to Significant Other.

Relive the moments ... recapture the memories.

Look now for the CENTURY OF AMERICAN ROMANCE series in Harlequin American Romance. In one of the four American Romance titles appearing each month, for the next twelve months, we'll take you back to a decade of the Twentieth Century, where you'll relive the years and rekindle the romance of days gone by.

Don't miss a day of the CENTURY OF AMERICAN ROMANCE.

A CENTURY OF
AMERICAN ROMANCE
1900's

The women...the men...the passions...
the memories....

CAR-1

Take 4 bestselling love stories FREE

Plus get a FREE surprise gift!

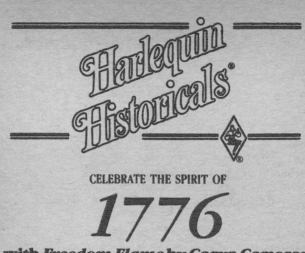

CELEBRATE THE SPIRIT OF

1776

with *Freedom Flame* by Caryn Cameron

Available in July 1990

What better way to celebrate the Fourth of July than with bestselling historical author Karen Harper writing as Caryn Cameron? *Freedom Flame* is a suspenseful tale of espionage and passion, set during our country's most exciting time—the American Revolution.

Meet George Washington and Benjamin Franklin, Benedict Arnold and John Andre. And, best of all, meet Meredith Morgan and Darcy Montour, who braved the dangers of British-held Philadelphia to spy for the American cause—and found a consuming passion that would bind them together forever.

Every reader will thrill to this sizzling story of the passionate man and woman who helped make our country free.

Only from Harlequin Historicals!

Harlequin Superromance®

Hamilton
H·O·U·S·E

A powerful restaurant conglomerate that draws the best and brightest to its executive ranks. Now almost eighty years old, Vanessa Hamilton, the founder of Hamilton House, must choose a successor.
Who will it be?

Matt Logan: He's always been the company man, the quintessential team player. But tragedy in his daughter's life and a passionate love affair made him make some hard choices....

Paula Steele: Thoroughly accomplished, with a sharp mind, perfect breeding and looks to die for, Paula thrives on challenges and wants to have it all . . .
but is this right for her?

Grady O'Connor: Working for Hamilton House was his salvation after Vietnam. The war had messed him up but good and had killed his storybook marriage. He's been given a second chance—only he doesn't know what the hell he's supposed to do with it....

Harlequin Superromance invites you to enjoy Barbara Kaye's dramatic and emotionally resonant miniseries about mature men and women making life-changing decisions. Don't miss:

- CHOICE OF A LIFETIME—a July 1990 release.
  - CHALLENGE OF A LIFETIME
    —a December 1990 release.
- CHANCE OF A LIFETIME—an April 1991 release.